THE
NEXUS RING

THE
NEXUS RING

MAUREEN BUSH

Edited by Laura Peetoom.
Cover painting by Aries Cheung.
Cover and book design by Duncan Campbell.
Printed and bound in Canada by Gauvin Press.

Library and Archives Canada Cataloguing in Publication

Bush, Maureen A. (Maureen Averil), 1960-
   The nexus ring / Maureen Bush.

(Veil of magic ; 1)
ISBN 978-1-55050-362-3

I. Title. II. Series: Bush, Maureen A. (Maureen Averil), 1960- .
Veil of magic; 1.

PS8603.U825N49 2007   jC813'.6   C2007-901255-8

10 9 8 7 6 5 4 3 2 1

available in Canada and the US from:
Fitzhenry & Whiteside
2517 Victoria Ave   195 Allstate Parkway
Regina, Saskatchewan   Markham, Ontario
Canada   S4P 0T2   Canada   L3R 4T8

The publisher gratefully acknowledges the financial assistance of the Saskatchewan Arts Board, the Canada Council for the Arts, the Government of Canada through the Book Publishing Industry Development Program (BPIDP), the Association for the Export of Canadian Books and the City of Regina Arts Commission for its publishing program.

To Mark, Adriene and Lia,
who played the game in the beginning,
read draft after draft,
and supported me through it all.
This is for you.

I KNEW FOR SURE THAT SOMETHING was wrong when I recognized the troll. I spun around to look at him as we drove away from the toll booth. He was staring at me with the nastiest glare I'd ever seen. We'd been travelling for seven hours, and I'd already seen him five times. I shivered, and muttered to myself, "This is not good, Josh." Why was he following us? And how did he get to the toll booth first?

CHAPTER ONE

THE QUEEN OF SAANICH

IT ALL STARTED WITH A STUPID GAME. MOM, Dad, Maddy and I were travelling home from Grandma's house in Metchosin. That's near the southern tip of Vancouver Island, west of Victoria. We live in Calgary, and every summer we drive out to visit Grandma. She has this fabulous art studio where I draw and paint every minute I can. My head was bursting with new ideas, and I couldn't wait to get home to work on them. But home was two long, hot days away.

To make the trip even worse, Dad made us get up early so we wouldn't miss the seven-o'clock ferry. But the traffic past Victoria and north to Sidney was awful. By the time we got to the ferry terminal at Swartz Bay, it was five minutes to seven.

"You might make it on the eight-o'clock ferry," said the woman selling tickets, her voice cheery.

Dad swore. "So much for my schedule," he grumbled. "This is the worst I've ever seen it."

The ferry terminal was packed with row after row of cars. Dad drove to the lane we were directed to, and parked at the end of another long row. Ferry staff keep everyone in order by time of arrival, unless you've paid extra to reserve a spot, which Dad always refused to do.

We got out of the van in the middle of the vast parking lot and organized ourselves for the wait. The sky was a beautiful clear blue, but a blustery wind tugged at our clothes. I pulled my navy hoodie over my T-shirt, and Mom handed Maddy her purple fleece. Dad was cranky because his schedule was messed up; I was cranky because Dad had woken me at 5:30 in the morning; and Maddy was asking, for the third time, "Mommy, when will we get home?"

Mom struggled to brush Maddy's hair into pigtails so it wouldn't tangle in the wind. She sighed, and spoke around the pink elastic in her mouth. "Tomorrow night, Maddy. Tomorrow night."

I could see her wondering how to get all these cranky people home without going crazy. She took the elastic out of her mouth and said, "Let's play a game."

"I Spy," said Maddy, leaping up and down. "Let's play I Spy."

"Stand still," said Mom, trying to hang on to Maddy's bobbing pigtail.

"I spy the seven-o'clock ferry leaving without us," I said.

"I spy my schedule ruined," Dad added.

Mom frowned at us. "Maybe something else." Her voice dropped to a whisper, and she waved her hands as she spoke. "I know why we missed the ferry. We don't have the right magic."

"What magic?" asked Maddy, already drawn into the story.

I rolled my eyes. Mom always makes up games. Last year was The Search for Unicorns. Actually, that was kind of fun, but I'm too old for that now. I'm almost twelve. Maddy's only seven; she adores Mom's games.

"There are veils of mist all along our route home, and we need something magic to pass through each one. Right now we need to find the right magic to get us onto the ferry."

"How do we find it?" Maddy asked.

"I don't know," said Mom. "That's the mystery. You and Josh will have to search until you each find something that feels just right."

There was no way she was building me into this game! I leaned into the van to grab my sketchbook and pencils.

We walked down the line of cars until we were as close to the water as we could get, near the huge ferry docks. While Maddy looked for something magic, I sketched the islands beyond the harbour.

A girl about my age walked up, looking out over the water. She had brown hair in long tight curls, and beautiful warm brown skin. I stared, wondering how to mix her skin colour from the watercolour paints Grandma gave me.

She looked up and caught me staring. I turned back to my sketch; she stepped closer to take a look. "Wow, that's really good," she said.

"Thanks," I muttered.

"The islands look like cardboard cut-outs sitting one behind the other." Then she laughed. "Sorry, that probably sounds really rude, saying your drawing looks like cardboard."

I grinned back. "No, it's okay. That's how I wanted them to look. That's how these islands always look to me."

She smiled, and we stood in silence. Desperate to say something, I said, "Where are you going?" just as she asked exactly the same thing. "You first," I said.

"Pender Island." She pointed across the ferry terminal to the Gulf Islands lineup. "I live in Nanaimo, but we're visiting friends on Pender for a few days."

"We were visiting my grandma in Metchosin," I said. "We're going to Tsawwassen." I pointed at the monster lineup and frowned. "Well, Vancouver. Calgary, eventually." I ground to a halt, feeling foolish.

Just then Maddy bounced up. "Josh, I found some magic!" She held up a white seagull feather. "It's perfect for our game – it'll help us fly across the ocean."

The girl smiled, but I didn't. "I'm not playing that stupid game," I said. "And I'm busy. Don't interrupt."

Maddy looked hurt. "Fine," she said as she walked away. "But it'll be your fault if we don't get on the next ferry."

I sighed, then carefully tore my sketch out of my sketchbook. I turned to the girl to ask if she wanted it, just as a man called out to her. "C'mon, Sam, time to go."

She raised a hand to him, then smiled at me, shrugged and walked away.

I was watching her leave when Maddy, Mom and Dad joined me.

"Did you find some magic?" Mom asked.

"No," I said, as I watched Sam get into her car. "I was just working on a sketch."

Mom looked disappointed.

Maddy said, "Josh doesn't want to play. He never wants to play with me anymore."

She sounded so forlorn I felt bad. I handed her the sketch. "Here's my magic. I just needed to finish it." It was almost worth not being able to give it to Sam, to see Maddy's face light up.

"Thanks," she said. "This is perfect."

We watched the Gulf Islands ferry load, then pull away from the far dock. Then the Queen of Saanich arrived and unloaded near us. Finally, we heard an announcement for boarding the eight-o'clock ferry to Tsawwassen.

As we wound our way through the lines of cars back to our van, Dad said, "Why is the Queen of Saanich here, instead of a bigger ferry? She's so small, and there are so many cars ahead of us, we'll never get on!"

"We'll get on, Daddy. I'm sure we have the right magic," said Maddy, waving my sketch and her feather.

We watched row after row of cars and trucks load onto the ferry, until I couldn't imagine any more squeezing on. Finally, our row started to move. Car after car crept down to the ferry, until it was our turn. Then the traffic guy put up his hand to stop us.

"Oh no!" said Dad. "*Two* hours off our schedule!"

"Maybe we *don't* have the right magic," said Maddy, worrying.

Then the traffic guy pointed at us, then at the ferry.

"Yes!" Dad yelled, and put the van back into gear.

I checked behind me. We were the last car to get on.

AFTER ANOTHER LONG LINEUP to buy breakfast on the ferry, we struggled through the crowded cafeteria with our plastic trays, to a table barely big enough for four. Mom started in on the game again. "We'll need more magic to get off the ferry," she said.

Maddy grinned; she loved this stuff. I dug into my waffles.

Dad leaned towards me. "Magic might be more fun than I Spy."

I shrugged him off, then thought about it. Maddy was going to keep bugging me. So was Mom. Maybe if I said yes they'd leave me alone. "What would I have to do?"

"You'll have to search for the right magic to take us through the next veil," Mom said. "Let your feelings help you."

I sighed. "Where do we look?"

"You could look in the gift shop."

The gift shop? Maybe I'd find something for an art project. I stifled my smile. "I guess," I said, with another sigh.

"What if we don't find the right magic?" Maddy asked.

Mom leaned towards Maddy and whispered, her eyes wide, "Then we'll be stuck on the ferry for another run. Three more hours."

WE FOUND A TINY GIFT SHOP tucked midway along the ferry. I groaned when I saw it. It was too small to have anything useful.

Mom gave us instructions. "Look around for something that might be magic. Trust your feelings."

"How will we know when we've found it?" Maddy asked.

"You'll know," Mom told her.

I snorted.

"Maddy's very intuitive, Josh," Mom said. "You should try it. Listen to that voice inside."

Mom is so weird. The only time my insides talk to me is when I'm hungry. "C'mon, Maddy," I said.

I browsed through the usual boring adult stuff – mugs and magazines and medicine. The only thing useful for art was an elastic band I found on the floor. As for magic, unless it was made in China, I wasn't going to find any in the kid section. Finally, I picked up a pen with a little ferry inside and slowly floated the boat to one end.

Maddy slipped past a tall woman in a black cloak and picked up something gleaming on the floor. "Look what I found." She tugged at my elbow. "Josh!"

I shrugged her off. "Just a sec!" She could never wait. I floated the ferry back while Maddy watched.

"That's so cute!"

Cute? I tossed the pen back in the box. "What do you want?"

Maddy showed me a green stone ring, dark in her small hand. "It was lying on the floor."

"You'd better take it to the clerk." I followed Maddy to the sales desk.

Maddy held out the ring to a young woman at the cash register. "I found this on the floor by the window."

"Oh, thank you, sweetie," said the clerk as she took the ring. "It belongs right here." She dropped it into a bowl of rings.

Maddy looked at the price on the bowl, then picked up the ring again. She slipped it on her finger and smiled. "This is what I'm going to buy."

I heard a gasp behind me and glanced over my shoulder. The tall woman in the cloak was staring at Maddy. When she saw me watching, she spun around and glided away. I turned back to Maddy. "I'll get some money."

It took a while to find Mom, lost in a book in the far corner. When I got back, a man was towering over Maddy, one hand reaching out to her. He was short and wide, with thick black eyebrows and huge ears. Maddy looked scared. She leaned away from him, a tightly closed fist behind her back.

I hurried to her side, and she grabbed me. The man scowled a black-eyebrows-meeting-in-the-middle scowl. I scowled back, trying to look just as fierce. He glared, then stomped out of the gift shop. I stared after him, my knees shaking. "What did he want?"

Maddy started waving her hands. "He wanted my ring. He offered to trade, but he scared me, so I said no."

"Good for you," I said. "Let's pay for the ring and get out of here."

"DID YOU FIND THE RIGHT MAGIC?" Mom asked as we walked out of the gift shop.

Maddy showed her the ring.

"This is lovely. What did you get, Josh?"

Oops. "I forgot. I didn't buy anything."

"You have to have something magic," Maddy said, "or we'll be stuck here. You have to." She stomped her foot, and Mom frowned at me.

Why was I stupid enough to agree to play? I looked around for something I could say was magic, then remembered the elastic. "Here," I said, pulling it out of my pocket. "I found this, I mean, it found me, just like your ring found you. So it must be magic." I smiled at Maddy, and she grinned back.

Our smiles are alike and we're both small, but otherwise, Maddy and I don't look much like brother and sister. She has straight golden brown hair that lightens every summer as her skin tans. The only parts of my skin that get dark are my freckles. I have pale skin and dark curly hair, like Mom's, only shorter. Maddy takes after Dad, except she has long hair, and he has hardly any.

"Dad said he'd meet us on deck. Let's go find him," Mom said.

The wind hit us as we stepped outside.

"I hope he found a sheltered spot," Mom grumbled.

"Are you kidding?" I said. "He always finds a quiet place so he can spread out his maps."

"There he is," said Maddy, and she dashed off to him.

Dad looked up and patted the life-jacket locker he was sitting on. We climbed beside him, tucked out of the wind and warm in the sun. Dad sat with an old brass compass in his hand and a map across his knees. "I'm plotting our route through the islands. Want to see, Josh?" Dad's a mapmaker. He always knows where he is, and he thinks we should, too.

"Where's your GPS?" I asked. Dad loves to use his Global Positioning System receiver to get satellite readings on our locations when we travel.

"I left it in the van. I'm going to do this the old-fashioned way. This was my father's compass. Want me to show you?"

"You know that stuff doesn't make any sense to me."

"I could teach you," he said. "I'll even get you your own compass."

"But I really don't care."

Dad sighed and turned back to his map.

I worked on sketches of the islands and the ocean until we neared Vancouver.

After a stop at the washrooms (Dad says travellers should pee whenever they get the chance), Dad led us down clanging stairs and through a heavy door to our car deck.

"Do you have your magic ready?" Mom asked. "Remember, if you didn't find the right things, we'll be trapped on the ferry."

"We'll just bounce against the veil and not be able to drive off," Maddy said.

Dad moaned. "That would put us *four* hours behind schedule."

Maddy held up her ring. "C'mon, Josh. Get out your elastic."

"All right," I said, sighing. I squirmed to dig it out of my pocket.

As Mom pulled forward to follow the line of cars off the ferry, something moved in the shadows. I glanced over and spotted the man from the gift shop. He caught me staring at him and scowled. I swallowed, my throat suddenly dry. "Look, Maddy," I whispered. "It's that man who wanted your ring."

Maddy turned and shivered. "He looks like a troll, lurking in the dark."

CHAPTER TWO

THAT MAN

WE STRUGGLED THROUGH VANCOUVER traffic, then sped past Fraser River Valley farms, towards mountains and fog. I sketched while Mom drove and Dad lectured about water.

"There's the Fraser River, flowing west to the ocean. Once we're over the Rocky Mountains the rivers flow east."

"How can a river flow in two directions?" Maddy asked.

Dad laughed. "It doesn't work that way, hon. Imagine the top of a mountain. When it rains or snows, water runs down the mountain. At the Continental Divide – that's the border between Alberta and British Columbia – water coming down one side of the mountain flows west to the Pacific Ocean, and water on the other side flows east."

"Wow," said Maddy, but she still looked confused. When her stomach growled, she shrugged and asked, "When's lunch? I'm starving."

"In just a few minutes," Dad said. "We're almost at Bridal Veil Falls, right on our revised schedule. We'll be home by dinnertime tomorrow, barring any construction delays, and we should have time for a swim before dinner tonight."

I checked my watch and sighed – twenty-nine hours to home.

Mom couldn't find the sign for Bridal Veil Falls, but Dad knew how to get there. It's a park with huge trees and picnic tables along both sides of a little stream.

We hauled a cooler to a picnic table by the water, where we ate sandwiches and Grandma's gingersnap cookies. The air was foggy and cool, and by the time we finished eating, our hair was covered with tiny drops of water.

After we ate, Dad made us walk up to the falls to stretch our legs. Mom started in on her game again. "There's another veil where we turn onto the Coquihalla Highway. You'll need something special from the falls. They're full of magic."

"The cokeawhata?" asked Maddy. "I can never pronounce that."

"The Coke ah hall ah," I said, making a face at her.

We followed the creek past huge mossy trees, drippy in the fog. Maddy picked up a pop can ring and offered it to me as my bit of magic.

"I don't want a useless piece of junk," I said.

Maddy stuck out her tongue, then shoved the metal ring into her pocket. Then she picked up a winged seed pod she pretended was a butterfly. She flew it over a wooden bridge and Mom roared, "Who's that walking on my bridge?"

Maddy shrieked, then giggled and took off after Mom. Mom raced up the path, but Maddy suddenly skidded to a halt. When I caught up with her, she was staring at the man from the gift shop, sitting perched in a rotted-out stump. I grabbed her hand and pulled her up the trail.

"Is he following us?" Maddy sounded scared.

He must be, I thought, trying not to look frightened. "Of course not," I said. "C'mon, let's catch up with Mom and Dad."

Maddy dashed off and I followed close behind. We raced through the forest, while I watched over my shoulder.

But I forgot about the man when we reached the falls. White threads of water poured out of the mist high above me. The forest smelled delicious, green and mossy. *Sap green*, I thought. *That's the paint colour I'd use.* I walked closer to the base of the falls, then looked at the pebbles below my feet. One, wet and grey, glistened at me. I dropped it into my pocket, then remembered that man.

I couldn't see Maddy anywhere. "Maddy? Maddy?" I tried to shout over the roar of the falls. I spotted a shadow hurrying down the path. That man? I raced after him, scared he'd got Maddy. "Maddy!" I screamed.

"booo!" Maddy yelled, jumping out from behind a tree.

"Aaah!" I screamed again. Then I bellowed, "Madd-dy!"

She left me alone after that, but I kept watch. As we headed down the trail I tried to tell Mom about the man, but she just laughed and said, "We'd better hurry, then. There's no way he'll be able to follow us through the next veil of mist."

I looked around as we drove away. In the shadow beside the bathrooms, the scowling man was watching us. Beyond the bathrooms, quiet in the trees, the woman from the gift shop stood watching him.

I SKETCHED SHADOWS to Mom's next magic veil, where Maddy made me hold out the rock I picked up at the falls. She flew her butterfly seedpod as the van curved north onto the Coquihalla, then waved her arms to mime bursting through a veil of mist.

"Yes!" Dad grinned and slapped his hand against

the steering wheel. "Right on schedule. How many more to go?"

"The next veil is at the toll booth halfway up the Coquihalla," Mom said.

"The troll booth," said Maddy. "It should be a troll booth!"

Mom laughed. "We'll need gold to get past a troll." She started to hunt for coins. "How much is it?"

"Ten dollars," Dad said. "Are you going to pay in change?"

"Sure. Trolls love gold, don't they, Maddy?"

Maddy wriggled in her seat. "Oh, yeah. And if we don't pay in gold, we can't get past him."

I interrupted. "Dad, I don't think this troll thing is very funny. There's this man we keep seeing; he looks like a troll. We saw him twice on the ferry and again at Bridal Veil Falls, and I think something's wrong."

Mom stopped me. "What did you say? He looks like a troll?"

"Yeah, that's how ugly he is."

"Josh, that's mean. I'm glad you're playing along with the game, but you can't make fun of people because you don't like how they look."

"But we keep seeing him. It's weird."

"Daddy, is he following us?" Maddy asked.

"No, of course not," Dad said. "Josh is just trying to make the game scarier."

Trust your feelings, Mom says, but everything's just a game to her. And Dad! He always knows where he is, but he hasn't noticed someone is following his kids. How could they not see?

I drew while I thought about it. We first saw that man in the gift shop, when Maddy was buying her ring. "Maddy, can I see your ring?"

Reluctantly, she passed it to me. The smooth, jade-green stone was still warm from her hand. I held it up to the light. There were no special markings; it was just a girl's ring. I sighed and handed it back.

We'd left the fog of the coastal mountains and were driving high up the Coquihalla. The mountains were small compared to the Rockies, but we were still high enough to be driving through clouds. Partway up the Coquihalla highway, we stopped behind a semi at one of the toll booths.

"Okay, guys," Dad said. "Will the troll like our gold?"

Maddy laughed. "He'll love it, and he'll have to let us through the veil of mist."

Mom poured loonies and toonies into Dad's hand. He pulled up to the booth and held out his handful of coins.

I gasped, then shrank back in my seat. The toll collector was that man from the gift shop! That's when I knew for sure that something was wrong. Slowly he reached out his hand; Dad poured the coins into his palm. He rubbed them while he gave Dad a receipt.

Maddy cheered. "Yes! It worked!"

The man twitched, leaned down and peered into the van. I looked back as we drove off. He was staring at us, his ears curled forward, his face twisted in a horrible scowl. I felt sick to my stomach. Why was he following us? And how did he get to the toll booth first?

I SKETCHED THE TROLL using one of my softest, darkest pencils. Then I drew the woman in the black cloak with a finer pencil, but I couldn't get it right until I deepened some of the shadows. Then I slept, and dreamed of a troll reaching for me.

Maddy woke me, cheering as we burst through Mom's veil of mist in Kamloops. Even with the air conditioner on, I was soaked in sweat. Maddy had curled my fingers around a water bottle for my part of the magic. I guzzled the warm water, then splashed some on my forehead. I checked my watch and groaned – still twenty-five hours to home.

The sun was blazing in a bleached-out sky. I pulled on my sunglasses. How could the sun be brighter here?

"Where's the next veil?" Maddy asked.

Mom thought about it for a minute. "I think it must be at the bridge crossing Shuswap Lake. Bridges and water are pretty powerful."

"What magic will we need?"

"Shuswap Lake? How about fruit? We'll stop at a fruit stand, and you and Josh can choose something to get us through the veil and feed us for supper."

I shook my head. Fruit is not magic. Water and rocks and even stone rings might be magical. But not apricots.

By late afternoon we had reached the Shuswap. We found a fruit stand and stocked up. For magic, Maddy scooped up a handful of blueberries and handed me an apricot. Just before we reached the bridge over Shuswap Lake, I took a huge bite out of it.

"Josh!" Maddy complained. "We'll be stuck if you don't do it right!"

I just ignored her. Soon we turned off the highway onto the winding road to the campground. Dad had been right; there was time for a swim before dinner. Maddy and I raced each other to the lake and splashed in. It was heavenly, cooling off after a long hot day. I lay on my back and floated, then jumped up with a start. What if that man followed us here? I kept watch after that, staying close to Maddy while she played, her red swimsuit gleaming in the sun.

After a dinner of hot dogs, mosquitoes, fresh peas and apricots, we roasted marshmallows. When we were full and sticky, Maddy got ready for bed while Mom and I cleaned up. Then Mom sat reading by the fire while Dad read to Maddy in the tent, and I paced, tossing my rock from hand to hand.

What if that man was still following us? He could sneak into the tent while we slept and – what would he do? I took a heavy flashlight to bed with me.

I woke in the middle of the night to total blackness, my heart pounding. What had woken me? Then I heard it. Rustling. A stick snapping. I touched the wall of the tent. I could feel it vibrating. Someone was out there.

I wiped the sweat off my hands, then grabbed the flashlight and held it tight. If it was that man, I'd smack him on the head. I lay staring at the door of the tent. I couldn't see a thing. I jumped at a slow "zzzup," the sound of the tent door zipper. I reached across Maddy to poke Dad with my left hand, and raised the flashlight in my right hand like a club. And then a train whistle rang out, startling me so badly I dropped the flashlight onto Maddy.

I heard scrambling and a twig crack, then silence around the tent as the train roared past the campground. I grinned. I hated being woken by trains in the night, but not this night. None of us would sleep deeply enough for that man to sneak up on us.

Maddy stirred. I whispered, "It's just a train, Maddy. Everything's all right."

DAD WOKE US AT SEVEN. Sunlight streamed through the tent door as he shook us. I yawned and stretched and checked my watch – only nine hours to home. I leapt out of bed and tugged on a blue striped T-shirt, yesterday's jeans, and my hoodie. It was warm enough for shorts, but I knew it would be cold later, in the mountains. Mom tidied Maddy's pigtails and hurried her into jeans and a pink T-shirt. I started stuffing sleeping bags with Dad, while Mom and Maddy cooked pancakes on the camp stove.

There was no sign of the man as we worked, and once we were in the van, I relaxed a little. Soon we'd left the lakes and heat of the Shuswap and moved into mountains lined with dark forests.

Mom planned the day's magic. "I think the other veils of mist will be at the Giant Cedars Boardwalk, the Rogers Pass, and the Spiral Tunnels. Those are all places of great power. And the last one will be the Banff Viewpoint, because we'll need a break by then."

I sat shaking my head. We always stop at those places. We should be called the "Same As Always" family. I was glad, though, when we pulled into the Giant Cedars parking lot. There's a boardwalk that winds up into the cedar forest, then down again in a long series of stairs. It's dark and mysterious.

It had just rained, so the air was cool and the picnic table wet. Mom dried it while Dad set out lunch. As soon as we'd eaten and packed away the leftovers, we headed for the wooden steps into the forest. Maddy dashed up the stairs, and I ran after her, still watching for that man. I made sure we didn't get too far ahead of Mom and Dad.

The steps wound up and up, with little landings in between, through a forest of trees so tall I couldn't see their tops, and trunks bigger around than I could reach. We heard a murmur, then a roar, of water. A stream rushed between rocks, trickled through a log-jam, then plunged down a waterfall.

We walked on, the boardwalk squeezing between trees. The clouds had broken up enough to let sunlight into the forest in gleaming lines. Maddy laid her cheek against the bark of a cedar tree where it was rubbed smooth by people's hands. Her hair shone gold against the deep red of the bark. My fingers itched to pull out my new watercolour paints and match the colours.

Mom and Dad passed us on the landing at the top of the boardwalk, holding hands and talking. I tried to get Maddy to keep up, but she dawdled, looking at trail signs, and when we finally headed down, a huge group of tourists was surging up the stairs. I plunged into the crowd, dragging Maddy behind me. Finally, we eased our way past and dashed down the steps. We leapt out of the forest into the picnic area. Mom and Dad weren't there.

"Maybe they went back in, looking for us," Maddy said.

We ran into the forest the way we'd come out, racing up the stairs, squeezing past the tour group, then leaping down the steps on the other side. We came back to the deserted picnic table, puzzled.

"Maybe they went to the bathroom and there was a lineup. Come on, Maddy. You know Dad."

They weren't at the bathroom. We wandered back to the picnic table. Still not there. "Maybe they're at the van," I said.

We crossed the road, searching.

"There," cried Maddy. "They're leaving. They're leaving without us!"

Our van was pulling out of the parking spot. We raced after it, screaming, "STOP, STOP!" and waving our arms. Mom and Dad didn't even glance around. They just drove off, looking dazed.

CHAPTER THREE

AS UGLY AS A TROLL

MADDY AND I STOOD IN THE ROAD, stunned. How could they leave without us? Maddy started to cry.

I hugged her, then stiffened. "Maddy," I whispered. "Look. That man. He's here!"

The man from the gift shop stood in the shadows by the boardwalk. He was grinning, a look much uglier than his scowl. We stared at him.

"Your parents won't be back," he announced. "Unless you give me that ring. Then I'll bring them back."

I glanced down at the ring on Maddy's finger. I couldn't believe what he'd said. How could he make people go away, and then bring them back?

Maddy yelled at him, "They'll come back. They won't leave us!"

"They just did! They think you're sitting in the back seats. I put two Shadows there. They look just like you, only they're a lot quieter."

"Shadows?" My voice squeaked. "What are you talking about?"

"Little pretend children. Very quiet. No trouble at all. And Shadows make people uneasy, so no one looks too closely. Your parents won't notice a thing."

Maddy slipped her hand into mine. I looked down at her; her eyes were huge and dark in her suddenly pale face. She whispered, "Josh, I'm scared. I want to go home."

Me too. I squeezed her hand. "It'll be okay, Maddy. I'll get you home. I promise." I turned to the man. "If we give you the ring, will you bring back our parents and leave us alone?"

He nodded, then reached out for the ring, fingers twitching.

"Josh, I don't think we should," Maddy whispered.

"What?"

"I don't like him. I don't think we should do anything he says."

"But don't you want to get back to Mom and Dad?"

"Yes, of course. But I don't think we should give him the ring."

The man stood, hand outstretched, scowling. Maddy scowled back.

"Maddy, we have to get back to Mom and Dad. Give him the ring!"

"I can't, Josh. It feels all wrong. I just can't do it."

"Maddy!" I wanted to tear the ring off her finger and fling it at the troll. What was her problem? A soft voice behind us made me jump.

"Maybe I can help."

Maddy and I turned and stared. The tall woman from the gift shop stood behind us, cloak swaying in the breeze.

"You were on the ferry yesterday," said Maddy.

"Yes," she said. "I can help you with this troll."

"What do you mean?" I said. "He's as ugly as a troll, but he's not really one."

"No?" She raised her left hand, palm towards the man, and wiped in a circle, like she was cleaning a mirror. "There. Now take a look."

Slowly, the man's face shifted. His nose grew larger and lumpier, his ears bigger, his skin rough. His body shifted too, becoming squat and lumpy. He looked meaner than ever. My stomach curled up on itself. Definitely a troll.

He glared at the woman. "Witch!"

She laughed, her dark eyebrows curving like wings. Even though she was wearing black, she didn't look like a witch. She looked more like a dancer, graceful in her long cloak, with her hair tied up at the back of her neck. Except, when I looked closer, I realized she was a little strange, not quite human, somehow.

She knelt by Maddy. "My name is Aleena." She gestured at the troll. "He wants your ring."

"Why?" Maddy asked softly.

"He uses it to travel, to steal gold. You mustn't give it to him!"

"But what should we do? Mommy and Daddy have left without us."

"I can help," Aleena answered. "I can take you to a place the troll can't go, and I can get you back to your parents."

"We're not supposed to go anywhere with strangers," Maddy said.

"Parents aren't supposed to drive off without their kids, either," I muttered. What should we do? Dad would say, "Use your head." But my head didn't know whether it was worse to leave with a stranger, or to stay with a troll. Mom would say, "Listen to your intuition, Josh." I tried, but all I heard was a voice screaming, "I don't know what to do!"

I had to pick something, and the troll was giving me the creeps. I took a deep breath. "Maddy, if you won't give your ring to the troll, I think we need to leave with Aleena."

"I guess…" Maddy said. She pushed her hand deep into her pocket.

As we turned away, the troll began to shake and stomp and roar. He screamed at us, "It's my ring. You stole it and I WANT IT BACK!!!"

Aleena ignored him. Maddy and I kept glancing back as we followed her to the far path into the forest.

"We can't go in there," I said. "The troll will follow us."

"Don't worry. We won't be here long."

We hurried to the top of the boardwalk, then Aleena stepped off the wooden path onto the forest floor.

"We're not supposed to go off the path," Maddy said.

"It's okay. You won't hurt anything. Just be careful not to touch these," she said, pointing to plate-sized leaves near the path. "That's Devil's Club. Its prickles can give you a nasty wound."

Maddy and I glanced at each other, then behind us, wondering where the troll was. Maddy's eyes were huge and dark. She looked terrified. I reached out to take her hand, then, together, we stepped off the boardwalk, eased past the Devil's Club, and followed Aleena into the forest.

We wound our way through the trees, stopping at a pair of huge cedars growing an arm's-length apart.

"Let me touch the ring," Aleena said.

Maddy held out her hand. Aleena's fist clenched as she reached for the ring, then slowly she opened her hand and touched the ring with one finger. She closed her eyes, took a deep breath, then gently blew out. As she exhaled, mist filled the space between the cedar trees. It deepened into a white glow, then a hole opened in the centre of the whiteness, a doorway in the mist.

Maddy and I watched with open mouths, then backed away.

Aleena stepped into the doorway, then held out a hand for Maddy. Maddy turned to me with wild eyes. I reached out to stop her, then heard pounding up the steps in the forest behind us.

We could hear the troll roaring, "STOP! That's my ring!"

Fear surged through me. I pushed Maddy into the doorway and jumped in behind her. I was immediately surrounded by a blanket of fog. I couldn't see anything behind me. In front, I could just make out Maddy, and the back of Aleena's head. The only sound was a strange whirring. I glanced at my watch; the hands were spinning wildly.

Aleena's head moved forward, out of the fog into dappled sunshine. I grabbed Maddy's shoulder, and followed her through the fog. It thinned, then cleared as we stepped out from between two cedar trees.

The forest was just like the one we'd left, except I couldn't hear the troll. As I looked around, I noticed other differences. The trees seemed more vibrant here, in richer greens, and there was more birdsong. I could hear other sounds more clearly too: water tumbling in the creek, wind in the branches, ferns rustling. When I walked on the spongy forest floor, the scent of moss and decaying cedar drifted up on the cool breeze.

The misty doorway was still open between the cedar

trees. Aleena said it would dissolve in a minute. She led us up the mountainside, over fallen giant cedars, past ferns as tall as Maddy. We stopped at the base of a waterfall plunging down in a deafening roar.

"If I'm to have human guests, I'll need a firestone," said Aleena as she stepped into the pool below the falls. She crouched down and ran her hands over the rocks lining the pool. Her eyes almost closed as she focused all her attention on her hands. Then, with a grin, she rose, her left hand closed. She opened her fingers and showed us a smooth stone, shining black with glints of gold.

"What is it?" I asked.

"Firestone. I'll show you later," she said, smiling. She slipped it into her cloak pocket. Then, as she stepped out of the creek, her smile vanished and the colour drained from her face.

Maddy and I turned to see what she was staring at. It was the troll, climbing up the mountainside, slipping through the shadows, fuming. My heart hammered as I turned back to Aleena.

"Gronvald! I thought I'd trapped him in the human world," she said. "He must have slipped through the doorway before it shut." She glanced around frantically. The troll had spotted us and was struggling up the slope. "Can you swim?"

"Yes," I said.

"A little," said Maddy.

"Just a little?" asked Aleena. "Okay, then not the creek." She hurried away, studying the forest floor. Maddy and I followed, while we watched the troll closing in, panting from the climb.

Aleena stopped by a puddle of murky water surrounded by moss. As the troll charged towards us, Aleena grabbed our hands and yanked us into the puddle. I stumbled, and as I fell, the moss became a forest and suddenly all of me was wet in the puddle that was becoming a lake. The water felt cool and trickly on my skin. We moved through it into darkness, flowing deep into the mountains. Blackness suddenly shifted to blinding light, even through my closed eyelids, and then, with a splash, we stopped.

CHAPTER FOUR

ALEENA, WATER SPIRIT

I OPENED MY EYES TO BRILLIANT SUNSHINE. Wiping water off my face, I looked up to a clear blue sky ringed by mountains. Dark trees lined the slopes of a valley surrounding a pale blue lake, where Maddy, Aleena and I stood in knee-deep water.

Where were we? There were no people, no cars, no boardwalk, and no towering cedars. I gazed around, awed. The trees radiated vibrant green, the water was a soft gleaming blue, and when I looked up at the mountains, the air shimmered.

I glanced at my watch, wondering if the hands were still spinning. They all pointed straight up – 12:00. That wasn't the time here; the sun was too low in the sky. I doubted we were anything close to five hours from home, either.

I thought magic was just pretend, but this wasn't Mom's crazy game. This was real. I swallowed, my throat dry in spite of the water all around me.

"Where are we?" I asked.

Aleena pointed to the nearest shore. "You'll be safe on that island. The troll hates water, and there are no caves or tunnels he can travel to."

"Couldn't he use a boat?" Maddy asked, nervous.

"I cast a water spell over the lake so he can't cross. A troll repellent for a repellent troll!" Aleena laughed, and her eyes laughed too. They were the deep blue of still water in sunshine. They would have looked peaceful, except for the flecks of dark grey.

We waded to the island, squelching through mud to the shore. Aleena led us through a small forest to a meadow filled with sunshine. The view was breathtaking; everything seemed to glow with energy.

Maddy looked like an otter, hair dark from the water, pigtails dripping onto her shoulders. I helped her peel off her clinging fleece, then tugged off my soaked hoodie and wrung it out.

Aleena slipped off her cloak. Her black pants and shirt were as tight as skin. She pulled her hair out of its bun, moving as if she had fewer bones in her body than humans do, like seaweed under water. Her hair fell past her waist, light grey at the crown of her head, gradually shading into black down her back. Then she shook herself, like a dog shakes

water off its fur. When she stopped, she was com-
pletely dry.

I shivered as I watched. I leaned down to take off
my water-filled runners. "What are you?" I asked, as I
struggled with the laces.

"I'm a water spirit," Aleena answered. "I can travel
through water. That's how I brought you here."

I yanked off my runners and poured water out.
"What do you mean?"

Aleena settled on the ground with her long legs
folded under her. She spoke in a low singsong voice,
like she was chanting an old story.

"I am Aleena, water spirit, daughter of the rain,
born of raindrops on moss. I have lived in this land of
ocean, lakes and rivers for many ages. It was peaceful
until the trolls came. They came for gold, over one hun-
dred human years ago. They are nasty, greedy creatures.
Many followed the hunt for gold north to the
Klondike, but some stayed here. That troll stayed."

Another shiver ran up my back. When I helped
Maddy dump out her runners, I could feel her quiv-
ering. "We need to get dry," I said. "We can't shake off
the water like you did."

Aleena nodded. "We'll light a fire."

Maddy and I squeezed our feet back into sodden
runners, then walked into the trees edging the meadow.
Aleena showed us how to find dead evergreen branches.
They broke off with a snap that reverberated in my ears.

"So," I asked, "how did the troll look human?"

"His name is Gronvald. He used a scrim to disguise himself."

"What's a scrim?" Maddy asked, huge eyes peering over her pile of branches.

"A scrim's an illusion that can be drawn around something to change how it looks. Humans expect to see other humans, not trolls, so it's easy for him to maintain a disguise. I washed it away to show you how he really looks."

"Did you use a scrim too?" I asked, watching her.

"No, I can't create scrims. I can hide myself in a fog, or wrap myself in a rainbow, but that wouldn't be much use on a ferry. So I just dressed myself to look human."

As we talked, we walked back to the meadow and stacked our branches.

"Clear a place for a fire," Aleena said, while she chose a handful of twigs.

Maddy and I brushed away leaves and branches, then set stones in a circle on the ground. When we were ready, Aleena laid her twigs in the centre, then reached inside her cloak and pulled out the firestone. It was translucent black, with gold threads lacing the inside. She wove her fingers in a dance around the stone, then drew out a golden thread of fire. I watched, astounded, as she danced the thread from her finger-tips over the pile of dead twigs. Soon they were smoking, then in flames.

"That's amazing!" I reached out for the stone. Aleena placed it on my palm with fingers like ice. I rubbed away her touch, then looked at the stone. I could see the threads inside, but all I could feel was a smooth coolness.

Aleena took it back, then gestured at the pile of branches. "You feed the fire. I'm better with water." She backed away towards the lake.

Maddy and I stoked the fire, then warmed our hands while our clothes steamed. We propped our runners on nearby rocks.

"Why is the troll following us?" Maddy asked in a small voice.

"He wants the ring," Aleena answered. "It's made of nexus stone. Gronvald uses the ring to travel to the human world to steal gold."

I shook my head. Dad always says we have to deal with whatever life puts in front of us, but I'm not sure he had this in mind.

"Our world is hidden behind a veil, like a curtain," Aleena said, "to protect our magic from humans. There are doorways in the veil. Magic folk can open them, but that drains some of their magic, and it takes weeks to recover. The ring makes it easier to travel back and forth."

I thought about Mom's "veils of mist." Had she actually known something all along? That was too weird. Shivering, I laid more wood on the fire. I felt chilled deep inside.

Aleena moved away as the fire grew hotter. Maddy and I stood with our backs to it, our clothes steaming.

"Where did the ring come from?" I asked.

"The ring was made by the giant at Castle Mountain for a child with a magic mother and a human father, so she could travel between worlds. After her father died, she stayed in the magic world, and gave the ring back to the giant."

Aleena stretched out on the ground. "When Gronvald learned about the ring, he set off a huge rock slide, then begged the giant to rescue the humans trapped in it. While the giant was away, Gronvald snuck into his castle and stole the ring."

Maddy started pacing as she listened. I felt like pacing too, but I didn't want either of them to know how nervous I was. I locked my hands behind my back and planted my feet near the fire.

"He used it to steal gold, but then he lost it," Aleena continued. "He was prospecting for gold, and crossed a marsh where moose were grazing. Moose hate trolls. When they saw Gronvald in their marsh, they attacked. He dropped the ring while running away, and the moose wouldn't let him come back for it. When I heard what happened, I searched the marsh and found the ring."

Aleena stretched, and smiled. "Gronvald's been trying to get the ring back ever since. He can smell it, somehow, and every time I cross between worlds, he follows. I travel through water, and he follows through caves and tunnels."

"Why do you want the ring?" Maddy asked.

"I use it to travel to the human world. I love human things – bathtubs and hot tubs and kayaks. But crossing between this world and the human world drains my magic too, so I use the ring to travel back and forth. It's easy with the ring." Aleena looked wistful.

Maddy and I moved around the fire so we could roast our fronts and still see Aleena. "So how did I get it?" Maddy asked.

I thought a scowl flashed across Aleena's face, but it disappeared so quickly I decided I'd been mistaken. "I was hoping to trap Gronvald. I thought the ferry would be a good spot for it. He'd be distracted by needing a scrim in the crowds of people, and by being so close to water. I left the ring near sunlight. If he'd leaned down to touch the ring, the sun would have turned him to stone."

"Forever?" Maddy asked.

"No, I'm afraid not." Aleena sighed. "He only needs twelve hours of darkness to thaw. I was going to move him to a sunny meadow where he'd be stone until fall. Instead, you picked up the ring." Her voice sounded tight.

"Why didn't you just say it was yours?" Maddy asked.

"Even dressed as a human, I don't look human. I didn't dare talk to anyone on the ferry." Aleena sighed again. "Gronvald won't let you keep the ring." She smiled at Maddy. "That's why you need to give it to me."

Maddy frowned. "Everyone wants to take my ring from me!"

Aleena's smile tightened. "Think about it for a while. You're safe here."

"We can't do that," I said. "Mom and Dad will be frantic."

"They won't know you're missing. Gronvald's magic is good. He put Shadows in your seats; your parents won't notice. And time shifts when we cross the veil. I can take you back to whatever time you want."

I picked up a stick and drew pictures in the dirt. I didn't understand any of this. How could Mom and Dad not know we were missing? How could time shift? And how were we going to get home?

Once we were dry, we walked through the forest to the far end of the island. A meadow filled with waist-high berry bushes stretched across the point of the island. A black mama bear and two cubs grazed on the berries. Watching them left me longing for Mom and Dad. I felt a surge of anger at Maddy for getting me into this. I turned away to hide it; I wasn't sure I wanted Aleena to know what I was feeling.

When I turned back, Aleena was laughing at the cubs. We watched them from the edge of the forest. They were cuddly fat bundles, faces sticky with berry juice, but Maddy and I both knew to stay away from them.

"What if they see us?" Maddy asked. "What if they try to…to…"

"To eat you?" asked Aleena.

"Yes," squeaked Maddy.

Aleena smiled. "They only come to the island for berries. If you want to pick some, I can make a spell to draw them away."

Maddy grinned. Berries are her favorite food.

"The smell of rotting fish should get their attention." Aleena walked to the shore, dipped her hands in the water, then laid them on the sand while she hummed an odd, tuneless song. Then she stood, wiped the sand off her hands, and joined us at the edge of the forest. We watched the bears amble over to the shore, sniffing and rooting around in the sand where Aleena had touched her wet hands.

"That'll keep them busy for a while," Aleena said, nodding towards the bears. "So eat your fill."

The berries were a deep purple-red, smooth and tangy like cranberries, but sweeter, with a dark aftertaste. Soon we were sticky-faced like the cubs, and red stained the front of Maddy's pink t-shirt. Aleena called the berries muskberries. I didn't understand why until I sniffed my hands. The juice smelled dark and heavy. Somehow the scent settled deep inside of me, and I could feel energy flowing to my fingertips.

When we'd finished picking berries, we hiked back to our end of the island. Aleena waded into the lake, crouched in the weeds and sat perfectly still. Her arms flashed out and she held up a struggling fish, silver in the late sun. Soon she had a pile of fish on the shore. She cleaned them, spitted them on a stick and roasted them over the fire for us. She left two raw for her own dinner. I had to turn away when she tore apart the raw fish with her teeth.

Maddy and I feasted on crispy fish, luscious berries, and the sweetest water I'd ever tasted. Usually Maddy won't eat fish, but she loved these. The sun set as we ate in a fiery blaze of orange and red, shading into purple in the twilight.

Aleena showed us how to use evergreen boughs to make a lean-to, facing the fire but not too close. Then we sat and watched the stars, Maddy and I warm by the fire, Aleena near the water.

I thought about camping trips in the mountains with Mom and Dad and how cold it got at night. And how icy the lakes were. "Aleena," I asked, "why isn't it colder here? And why didn't we freeze in the lake?"

Aleena smiled. "The magic protects us, just a little. From winter storms, cold at night, icy water. It gives us pockets of warmth when we're sleeping or swimming, so we need less fire and clothing and buildings, all those human things."

I wasn't going to complain, lying outside at night, warm by the fire, happy under the stars. The lake shimmered in the moonlight, reflecting the sparkling night.

"The sky looks different here, too," I said. "There are so many stars, and they're so bright."

"Humans do things that weaken magic," Aleena said. "This is how stars really look."

"Oh yeah," I said. "There's no light pollution here."

"Yes, but it's more than that. In your world stars are just objects in the sky. They're a living part of our world."

I had no idea what she meant, and then one of the stars winked at me. I looked closer and it was still, but it made me smile.

I lay back, drinking it in. The sky was deep blue-black, with a gazillion stars scattered across, some in brilliant clusters, others shining alone. They took turns sparkling, first one then another across the sky, as if they were talking to one another.

As the fire died down, Aleena left to sleep near the water. Maddy and I sat staring at sparks dancing into the night like tiny shooting stars, until Maddy leaned against me and fell asleep. I settled her in the lean-to, then lay beside her, trying to tease apart my tangle of emotions. I was longing for home, and afraid of that awful troll, and worried about Mom and Dad, and weighed down by responsibility for Maddy, and at the same time this beautiful world filled me with excitement and awe. Finally, I gave up trying to figure it out, and just lay watching the stars.

CHAPTER FIVE

STORM CLOUDS

S QUAWKING BIRDS WOKE ME. I STUMBLED around in the early light coaxing the embers of our fire into flames. The air smelled sharp, like a cold new apple. Mist rose off the water, but the sky above was a luminous blue. Maddy and I peed in the bushes, then washed in the lake.

Aleena caught more fish for breakfast. Last night, fish had been wonderful, but I'd rather have toast first thing in the morning.

Just as I was choking down my last bite, the ground started to shake, a low rumbling beneath my feet. I looked around. The shimmer of the mountain across the lake faded, leaving it dull and slightly greyed. Then the rumbling stopped, and the greyness vanished.

"What was that?" I asked Aleena. "That rumbling?"

"There was a train in the tunnel in that mountain." She pointed across the lake. "Humans cut two tunnels in the mountains for trains to spiral through, because the pass is so steep. And when a train is in the tunnel in the human world, we can feel it rumbling here."

"What happened to the light on the mountain? It faded, and turned kind of grey."

Aleena closed her eyes for a moment. "The veil can't keep out human changes that reach deep into the earth, like tunnels. They touch our world, and they weaken our magic."

Quietly, we finished eating.

As soon as we were done, Aleena leaned back and said, "It's time to talk about the ring. What do you want to do?"

Maddy sighed. "What I want more than anything is to get home."

Aleena smiled. "Give me the ring and I'll take you home." She walked over to Maddy and held out her hand. Her fingers trembled.

Maddy pulled the ring off her finger, then hesitated.

"Give me the ring," Aleena said.

Maddy frowned and tightened her grip. "No. Everyone wants to take my ring from me, but I'm going to keep it." She glared at Aleena.

What? How could she not understand? We needed Aleena to help us get home! I jumped up. "Maddy, let's get more firewood." I turned to Aleena. "I'll talk to her."

Maddy and I walked into the forest. I growled at her, "What is your problem?"

"Something doesn't feel right."

"Oh, Maddy, not again! First the troll, now Aleena?" I snapped dead branches with great bursts of anger.

"Josh, when I think about giving it to her, I get a stomach ache. And when I think about not giving it to her, I feel better."

"Aleena just wants the ring so she can visit our world and go kayaking and stuff. What's wrong with that?"

"I don't know!" Maddy wailed. "I just feel it. I don't want to keep the ring, but I can't give it to Aleena. I don't know what to do."

"Just give her the stupid ring!"

Maddy glared at me. I glared back. Arms full of branches, we faced each other, like we sometimes do in staring contests. Except this wasn't a game. Finally, I threw down my branches and stomped off. Maddy can be so stubborn! She *had* to give the ring to Aleena so we could get back to Mom and Dad!

I watched her struggle with her branches while I worried about what to do. I shoved my hands into my pockets and banged a finger on the rock from Bridal Veil Falls. I pulled it out and looked at it. What I needed was a compass like Dad's, right in my pocket. But not for finding north. I needed one to help me figure out what was the right thing to do. Maddy always seemed more sure than I was. I sighed and tossed the rock away. Maybe she really did know something I didn't. Maybe I could stall a little, to give us time to figure it out.

I walked back to Maddy. "Okay, I'll tell Aleena you need some more time."

Maddy smiled in relief and followed me back to Aleena.

Aleena watched us as we carried wood into the clearing. "Are you ready?"

I spoke quickly. "Maddy doesn't want to give up her ring yet. We'd like to spend more time here. Maybe you could show us some magic."

Aleena stood perfectly still. Her pale skin, almost blue in the shadows, looked colder. Her eyes narrowed, and her voice deepened. "Give it to me. Now."

"No," said Maddy.

"GIVE IT TO ME!"

"No!"

Aleena's eyes darkened, and she raised her arms to the sky.

I stepped forward, ignoring my wobbly knees. "I'm sure she'll be ready soon, but…" I stopped as Maddy pointed over my head. I looked up and saw black clouds churning and growing.

Her face dark with rage, Aleena danced her hands across the sky, building clouds, raising a howling wind. The sky turned black as clouds boiled above us. Lightning leapt from mountain peak to mountain peak. Thunder filled the valley.

I felt paralyzed. Maddy shuddered, but thrust her hand deep into her pocket.

Aleena roared, "I want that ring. You won't keep it from me, you little brat. I WANT IT NOW!" Her thunder crashed back and forth across the valley.

I stared, frozen. "Maddy, give it to her. Maddy…"

"No."

"Maddy, you're only seven years old. Give her the ring!"

"No!"

Maddy faced Aleena, shaking but stubborn, with me beside her. Aleena stared at us, lightning and thunder ripping up the sky behind her. We stood like that for what seemed like hours, until Aleena lowered her arms, and the thunder and lightning subsided. The clouds settled into a dark ceiling, not as wild as before, but still ominous.

Aleena glowered at us, her eyes dark as the clouds. "If you won't give it to me, I'll just have to take it!"

Maddy backed away.

"Give me the ring," Aleena ordered, stepping closer.

"No," Maddy shouted, and she darted to the far side of the fire.

Aleena followed, closing in on Maddy, who jumped out of reach. Aleena stalked her around the fire. Maddy looked more and more frantic.

I grabbed a burning branch, and stepped between them. "Stop," I said.

Aleena stopped. I moved forward, and she backed away, never taking her eyes off the fire in my hands. She jumped to the side, trying to get around me to Maddy, but I thrust the branch at her. She stepped back, panting. I kept pushing her back, to the edge of the lake.

Her face grew angrier and angrier, until she stepped into the water and said, "Let's see how you like it here on your own, with just the bears for company!" Then she dove into the lake.

I stood staring at the ripples where Aleena had disappeared.

"I should have given her the ring," said Maddy, sniffing.

"Yes," I said as I watched the ripples vanish. "You should have given her the ring. You should have given the troll the ring!" My voice rose as I burnt off my fear in anger. "You should never have picked up that awful ring in the first place! And you should never have involved me in your stupid game with Mom. But you did, and now we're stuck here, and I'm the one who has to rescue us!"

By the time I was done, Maddy was sobbing. I didn't care. I stomped into the forest, smashing past branches and leaping over fallen logs.

I crashed through the forest all the way to the berry patch, then stood watching the mama and her cubs eating together. After a while, the anger eased out of me, and I started to feel lonely – and really, really mean. When the bears left, I did too.

I walked back to Maddy, knelt and hugged her. "I'm sorry," I said. "You knew something was wrong." I held her until she stopped crying.

"But what are we going to do?" Maddy said, sniffing. "She's left us here all alone."

"We're not alone," I said. "We have each other. We'll figure this out together."

CHAPTER SIX

TRAPPED

MADDY LOOKED UP WITH TEAR-SOAKED eyes, waiting for me to come up with a plan. I turned away, overwhelmed by the pressure. I would get us home. I just had to! But how?

I started sketching down my pant leg, and as my hand worked, my brain did too. "Let's pick some berries," I said, "and we can check how many are there."

Maddy felt better as soon as she was eating. I just kept worrying about Aleena. I remembered drawing her – how I had to use a dark pencil and deepen the shadows before I was satisfied. I should have known not to trust her.

Finally, I nibbled some berries. Energy surged through me, but something was making me nervous. I scanned the meadow. There was Maddy, a dark back bending over a bush. Except Maddy was wearing pink. I looked again. Beside it was another dark back. Bear cubs. Just then Maddy stood, right across the berry bush from the cubs.

Choking back a yell, I looked across the meadow, trying to spot the mama bear. I couldn't see her, but I knew she'd be nearby. Dad taught me you never, ever, want to get between a mama bear and her cubs.

I had to get Maddy out of there. If I walked straight to her, I'd be moving towards the cubs, too. I might alert the mama. Instead, I moved towards the shore. Then, in a low voice, I called to her. "Maddy!"

She looked up. So did the bear cubs.

"I need you to walk straight to me, right now." She started to speak but I put a hand over my mouth and shook my head. Maybe she saw the urgency in my face, because she began walking towards me without arguing.

"That's it," I said. "Slowly, right to me." I still couldn't see the mama, but she had to be nearby. I kept looking. A movement at the edge of the trees gave her away; mama was coming. "Come on, Maddy," I murmured.

She reached me and whispered, "What is it?" I shook my head and took her hand. We walked along the shore until we were almost out of sight of the bears. Then we turned, and I pointed to the berry patch. The mama bear had joined her cubs and was standing on her hind legs, watching us. I could hear her growling. We kept walking.

"I don't think we can stay here," Maddy said.

"Are you ready to give Aleena the ring?"

"No," she said in a small voice. "I just can't! It's not right."

"Can you give the troll the ring?"

"No," she said, in a smaller voice.

"Then we'll have to find our own way home."

Maddy whimpered. "I'm scared."

I swallowed my fear. "I know, but I have an idea. What if we can find one of the doorways between the worlds? Maybe we can open it with the ring."

"Maybe – but where do we look?"

I pointed to the mountain across the valley. "Aleena said one of the Spiral Tunnels runs through that mountain. I think we could hike to it. A tunnel would be a good place for a doorway, since the tunnels already link our worlds."

"But what about Aleena, and the troll? Won't they try to follow us?"

"Aleena expects us to stay here. And we'll bring a torch, to fight her off."

"And the troll?"

"I don't know. Maybe we can go really fast, so he can't keep up."

Maddy didn't look convinced, and I didn't feel it, but I couldn't think of another plan, so we set to work.

We built up the fire and put the end of a thick branch in the flames. Then we stripped down to our underwear. I stuffed our clothes and runners into my hoodie, then we walked down to the lake. We found a log floating near the shore. I held it steady while Maddy scrambled on. When I let go, the log rolled, dumping Maddy into the water.

"I guess you can't carry the clothes," I said.

"No kidding," she muttered, wiping water from her eyes.

I found a second log, and tied them together with our pants. Then Maddy climbed on top. She held the rest of our clothes in my hoodie, and waved the burning stick in the air. "Let's go," she said, pigtails dripping.

"Easy for you to say," I grumbled as I swam, pushing the raft ahead of me. Every time something brushed against my legs, I thought it was Aleena. I'd surge forward, then tire and rest. Then something else would brush past me and I'd be off again, struggling to push the raft as fast as my racing heart would let me. By the time we reached the shore of the lake, I was exhausted.

Maddy untied our pants and wrung them out, then put her own clothes back on. I pulled on my dry T-shirt and hoodie, then struggled into wet jeans.

I picked up the smouldering torch and we set off. We oozed through mud to the edge of a stream, then waded across. The water washed off the worst of the mud, but soon we were walking through more on the other side.

Squelch, ooze. Squelch, ooze.

Finally the ground rose, and we found a fallen tree to perch on. We tried to bang off the mud, but it just splattered up our legs and onto our hands. We wiped our hands on some leaves and kept walking. It had to get better after this.

It didn't. Maddy wanted to follow the creek, but I insisted we walk along the flank of the mountain, so I could spot the tunnel. Except that took us straight into dense forest. We pushed our way through the trees, getting scratched and tired and more and more confused. I longed for Dad, or at least for his compass, a map and a lesson on how to use them. Finally, we sat on a boulder to rest.

"I don't know where we are," I said. "I can't see anything from here. Maybe I should climb those rocks, so I can look around."

Maddy looked at the rock face I was pointing to, then at me. "Josh, you don't know how to rock climb."

"I can try," I said. I handed Maddy the torch, then started climbing. The rock face was like a little cliff in the middle of the forest. I climbed quickly at first, then, when I realized how high I was, more carefully. Somehow I managed to pull myself high enough to see above the trees. To my right, the forest opened into sunshine, and I could see a mountain across the valley. I grinned. That must be where the second tunnel spiralled. Now I knew where we were! But as I looked to the left my grin faded. I started sliding down the rock face.

"Maddy, the troll is coming," I whispered. "Run, through there." I pointed to the right, into the forest. "Get into sunlight."

Maddy stood, waiting for me.

"Run!" I said. "I'll be right behind you."

She dashed off as I clambered down the rocks. Soon I was pounding along behind her. I could hear the troll cursing as he crashed through the forest. And then I heard Maddy scream.

"Maddy, where are you?"

I burst out of the trees, then slid to a stop, teetering on the edge of a cliff. I peered down. Maddy was clinging to a ledge partway down the cliff, her legs dangling.

"Hang on, Maddy, I'm coming!" She twisted around to look up, but I shouted, "Don't move. Just hang on. I'll be right there."

The cliff was steep, but not vertical. And it was in the sun, so the troll couldn't reach us. I could hear him, though, cursing at the edge of the forest.

I lowered myself over the edge, aiming just to the left of Maddy. Slowly I worked my way down the cliff face. All the while I talked to Maddy, trying to sound like Dad. "Hold tight, Maddy. I'll be there in a sec." My foot slipped and I almost fell. I bit my tongue to stop myself from crying out. I could taste blood.

Finally I could feel the ledge under my right toe, and I eased down to it. It was barely wide enough to stand on, but it widened towards Maddy. I worked my way along it, then sat with my back braced against the wall and grabbed Maddy. With me pulling and Maddy scrambling, she wiggled up beside me.

We just sat there a while, Maddy filthy and scratched and scared, me with torn hands and bleeding tongue, heart thumping. Dark clouds rolled in, blocking the sun. All the time I was climbing, I was focused on getting to Maddy. But now, safe for the moment, words banged around my head like bumper cars. *We'll never get down – the troll will catch us – we'll never get home.*

Finally Maddy took a huge breath, blew it out, and said, her voice quavering, "I was so scared. I thought I was going to fall all the way."

"I know," I said. "You were really brave. Now you need to be brave again, so we can climb to the bottom."

Maddy looked way down between her feet, then at me, horrified. "I can't, Josh. I just can't!"

"You have to," I said. "We can't go back; the troll is up there. So we have to go down. I'll help you. We'll do it together."

Maddy shut her eyes and took another breath. Then she nodded.

I tried to sound confident, but I almost threw up when I lowered myself from the ledge and hung, groping for a foothold. Then I had one. I worked my way down to another ledge, then called to Maddy. "C'mon, it's not so steep."

Maddy's pale face peered down at me. She whimpered, then turned and slowly wiggled over the edge. I told her where to put her feet, then reached up to hold an ankle. "That's it. Now to your left, a little further. Sure you can reach it. C'mon. You can do it."

And then she was beside me, trembling and looking sick.

Slowly we worked our way down the cliff face, from ledge to ledge, until the steepness eased into a gentler slope.

We were surrounded by towering mountains, tan and red-brown and grey, with patches of snow near the peaks, and trees covering the slopes. Below us a river carved through the valley floor. It was milky white and roaring. The air was warm, with a cool breeze that smelled of ice and sweet spruce.

Even though I was scared and confused, I stood for a moment in awe at the beauty of it. I longed to paint it, to try to capture all the colours of the rocks. I looked carefully, trying to memorize the details. I wanted to draw and paint everything as soon as we got home. If we got home.

We found our torch at the bottom of the cliff. The tip had broken off, and the fire gone out, so now we had no protection from Aleena. And I didn't think the troll was going to stay at the top of the cliff hoping we'd come back. We had to find a doorway quickly.

"Remember last year, Maddy, when we stopped near here and Dad explained about the Spiral Tunnels?"

Maddy shrugged. "I just remember being disappointed because there was no train."

I grabbed a stick and drew a long line, from west to east. "This is the railway line from Vancouver to Calgary." Then I drew a figure eight, pointing north. "The track makes a figure eight pattern, curving first through that mountain," I pointed to our right, "that's north of the rail line, then across the valley to the mountain on the south side," I pointed to the left, "where it curves through another tunnel. And all along the way, the track gets higher and higher."

"But why?" asked Maddy.

"The mountain pass is really, really steep. This is a train's way of zigzagging up a hill too steep to run straight up." I scanned the mountain across from us. "There must be tunnel openings in this world," I said, trying to guess where they might be. Then I spotted one.

"Maddy, see that dark hole?" I pointed across the valley. "That's the entrance to one of the spiral tunnels. The other end is..." I scanned the mountainside, "there, higher up the slope. And there's another tunnel on this side of the valley, in the mountain behind us."

We turned and searched. I knew roughly where the openings had to be, but could we find one?

"Do you really think we can find a doorway in one of the tunnels?" Maddy asked.

"We'd better – before the troll or Aleena catch us!"

We headed up the mountainside, scrambling through the trees, searching for the nearest tunnel opening. I kept watching for the troll and Alcena.

Maddy found the tunnel. She was climbing a bit to the left of me, and walked around a tree growing right in front of it. The opening was tall, round and smooth. We groped our way inside, panting from the climb, and tried to guess where a doorway might be. All I could see of Maddy were huge eyes, white in the darkness, and a bit of light gleaming on the gold in her hair.

"Hold out the ring," I said. I touched it with one finger. "Let's do what Aleena did – close your eyes, take a deep breath, then exhale."

I closed both eyes, sucked in a big breath, and tried to imagine mist forming as I blew out. I couldn't feel any mist; I just felt stupid. I opened my eyes to see Maddy puffing her cheeks, then blowing out in a great whoosh. Rock dust rose from the walls of the tunnel and choked us. That was as misty as it got.

"We have to find the doorway," I said. "The troll could be here any moment."

"And he is," a voice growled.

Maddy screeched and grabbed my hand. We heard footsteps, then watched a shadow emerging from deep in the tunnel.

"And now," said the troll, "it's time to give me MY RING!" He was bellowing as he finished.

"We're not going to give it to you," I said, trying to sound brave as I pushed Maddy behind me towards the entrance. "And once we're outside in the sun, you can't come near us."

And then a shadow blocked the entrance to the tunnel, a tall, lean shadow, and Aleena's voice called out, "The sun doesn't bother me."

Maddy moaned and leaned against me. "How could she find us?"

"I followed your scent through water," she sneered. "I knew the moment you stepped into the lake. It just took a while to track you here."

Aleena stepped towards us, while the troll screamed from the shadows, "It's my ring. Don't give it to her, give it to me!"

Stomach churning, I tried to come up with a plan. If we could get outside, the troll couldn't follow us, not into sunshine. Then even that hope was snatched away, as the sunlight outside the tunnel vanished behind a cloud.

I could feel Maddy moving behind me. Her hand rose, and something flew from it, high into the air, over Aleena's head. I heard it ping off the roof of the tunnel, then bounce into the shade just outside the entrance.

"What was that?" I asked. "Was it the ring?" I could hear panic in my voice. The troll and Aleena heard it too.

"Yes, I threw the ring," Maddy said, with a voice full of determination. "You can have it! All it does is cause trouble."

Aleena spun around and raced outside. The troll roared past, slamming us against the tunnel wall. He slid to a halt at the entrance of the tunnel, then stepped out into the shade of a dark cloud.

Quietly, Maddy and I followed them out of the tunnel, then slipped off to one side. The troll and Aleena searched the ground frantically, both on hands and knees. Maddy and I crept a little further away. Aleena leapt, as she spotted something lying in the grass. The troll was just a step behind. Aleena reached out, closing her hand over it, and the troll's hand closed over Aleena's.

Just at that moment, a single ray of sunshine shone through the clouds and touched the troll's hand. He stared in horror as his hand turned to grey stone. The greyness crept up his arm, then down his body and up to his head. Within moments, the troll was a stone statue.

Aleena screamed in rage, her hand caught in his fist of stone. "Look what you've done," she cried. "Help me!"

"Josh," Maddy said. When I turned to her, she opened her hand, showing me the ring nestled in her palm.

"But what did you throw?" I asked, astonished.

"The useless piece of junk pop-can ring in my pocket," she said, with a mischievous smile.

"Maddy!" I grabbed her and spun her around. "You're brilliant! We're safe for twelve hours!"

Aleena screamed at us, her face distorted. "You'll never get away with this."

Maddy smiled as she slipped the ring onto her finger. "Let's get out of here."

As we turned our backs, Aleena yelled after us, "Only magic folk can cross the veil. You need me, and I won't help until I get that ring!"

CHAPTER SEVEN

THE OTTER-PEOPLE

MADDY AND I WERE SO PLEASED WITH ourselves, we raced downhill in great leaps. Aleena had said the troll needed twelve hours out of the sun to thaw, so we were free of them for at least that long. Parts of the valley were in shadow as the sun moved across the sky. It was maybe five o'clock in the afternoon, so we had until early in the morning to get home.

We wound our way between towering trees, found an animal track, and followed it to the riverbank. I stood looking around, trying to orient myself. "There's a road here in our world," I said. "Maybe there's a doorway nearby."

We wandered around taking turns holding the ring,

inhaling and exhaling, but we couldn't find a doorway or any other link to our world.

"Maybe we should climb up to another tunnel," I said, frustrated.

"Or maybe we just can't find a doorway by ourselves," Maddy snapped.

"Yeah, well, I'm not going back to Aleena! There must be another way." I squatted on the bank of the river and tossed rocks into the water. The sun was warm on my back, but cold air rose from the river, chilling my hands.

Maddy settled beside me. "Josh, I have this feeling."

"Not another one of your feelings!" I groaned.

"I think there's another way. I don't know what, but I don't think we have to go back to Aleena."

"Oh great. So what do we do? Just sit here and wait for it to fall on us?"

Maddy flushed and hung her head.

I sighed. "I'm sorry."

"No, you're right. What's the good of a feeling like this if it can't help? What I want more than anything is to get home, and we can't!" She shrugged in frustration, then froze.

I glanced down at her. She was staring to the left, where a cluster of trees grew near the riverbank. I turned to look. Several creatures were playing on the shore. They were like people, but they looked sleek, like otters, and were covered in fine fur. Two were hard to see in the shade. Sunlight shone on the third, the tallest, on auburn fur and the soft tan skin of its hands and face. It was about Maddy's height, but thinner, with a small mouth and ears, and a pointy nose. Its eyes were round and dark, its feet flat and wide at the toes. There was fur in a vee down its forehead, ending in a point near the bridge of its nose.

Maddy and I stayed still as statues, hardly breathing. I mentally sketched them – two tall and one small, fine pencil for delicate features, soft shading for the fur. And then, over the roaring of the water, a new roar emerged. I jerked up, trying to trace it.

Maddy poked me. "You moved. Now they see us!"

I glanced back along the river. The creatures stared at us, startled. The roaring grew, and the ground began to shake. I could see dust billowing on the mountain-side behind us. Roaring filled my ears and rocks bounced past us. It was an avalanche!

I leapt up and grabbed Maddy, but a rock slammed into me. Pain flared up my leg, and I collapsed. Maddy pulled me to my feet and dragged me clear as rocks flooded down the mountain like water. A boulder crashed to the ground where Maddy had been sitting, then bounced into the river in a great spray of water. Rocks thundered down for what seemed like hours, but was probably only a few minutes. Finally, the river of rock slowed, then stopped.

We coughed on thick dust and waited for the air to

clear. As the dust settled, we could see a scar up the mountainside, the trees buried under grey rock. The avalanche had reached a finger into the river, but the water just flowed around it, tumbling and cold. We stared at where we'd been sitting. It was buried in boulders.

My little sister saved my life! Even though I was just thinking it, I could hear my voice squeak. Maddy saved me! I looked at her with new respect; she was small, but she was brave.

Then Maddy cried out and started to run. "Those creatures!" she gasped, as she climbed the rocks. "The otter-people!"

I stood gingerly, testing my leg. It was wet with blood, but I could stand on it. I gritted my teeth, trying to ignore the pain, then hobbled after Maddy. I scrambled over rocks, dreading what we'd find. As we drew closer, we heard a soft keening filled with grief.

When we came around a pile of rocks, we could see the tall otter-people, covered in dust and blood, pushing at a boulder while a soft whimpering came from underneath. They spoke to each other in whistles and hums while they struggled to move the boulder. Maddy and I ran up; they backed away in fear.

"Is your little one under here?" asked Maddy gently.

I knelt, and peeked under. The boulder was balanced on a pile of rocks, and there was a gap underneath. I could see a little hand, and hear crying.

The boulder was almost as tall as I was. I put my shoulder to it and shoved. Maddy and the otter-people joined me, and we pushed together. The boulder didn't move. We pushed again and again, but we couldn't shift it.

The whimpering stopped. The otter-people began sobbing, frantically digging at the rocks around the boulder. I worried that if they pulled out a rock, the boulder might slip lower and crush the child. I glanced around and spotted broken trees, smashed in the avalanche.

"Maddy, help me," I called out as I ran to a strong branch. "I need…this…branch…" I gasped as I struggled to free it from a tangle of trees and rocks. Finally we yanked it out, and raced back to the boulder.

"A lever," I said, trying to explain. I jammed one end as far under the boulder as I could, then grabbed the other end, and pulled down. The wood groaned, but the boulder stayed put. Maddy and the otter-people joined me, and we all pulled down on the branch. Slowly, the boulder began to shift, just a little, then a little more, and then with a crack the branch broke, the boulder settled back, and we tumbled to the ground.

I raced off for a stronger branch, jammed it under the boulder, and we all pulled again. Slowly, the boulder shifted, a little, then a little more, and then it rolled away from us with a great rumble. The branch came free and we fell again.

Maddy and I stood slowly, to give the otter-people time to reach the child. The auburn one stood as the other knelt and gently lifted the otter-child. She crooned to it, tears running down her cheeks. The little one opened its mouth and let out a cry just like a human baby squawking, then it hiccupped and started to sob.

I blinked back my own tears as Maddy and I grinned. What I could see of the face, around the wailing mouth, was warm brown, surrounded by golden fur. The otter-person holding it had the same warm brown skin, with deep brown fur. I pulled off my hoodie and helped wrap the otter-child in it. Its crying slowed as it nestled into the blue fleece, still warm from my body.

The auburn otter-person turned to us. It spoke in a soft whistly voice. "Humans saved Godren. I thank you." It bowed its head and made a sort of growly purr, *chrrr*.

I bowed back, awkwardly.

Maddy bowed and smiled. "I'm Maddy."

Four long fingers reached out. "You are female, Maddy?"

Maddy nodded, and held out her hand.

"I am Eneirda. Female." They touched fingers, and stood still for a moment, then both nodded and turned. "They are Arnica, female, and her child Godren, male." Then she looked at me expectantly.

"Uh, Josh. My name is Josh. Uh, male." I stammered a little.

The otter-person softly touched fingers with me. "How can you be here? *Sssst!* There be no humans in this world. Are you not human?"

"Yes," I said, surprised. "We're human."

Maddy whispered to me, "Tell her about the ring."

"No," I said. "Shh."

Maddy pushed the ring deeper into her pocket.

Eneirda watched while we whispered. When we were done, she nodded. "Come to camp. *Chrrr.* Godren needs healing." She turned and headed downstream, away from the avalanche. Arnica followed, carrying the still crying Godren.

"Should we go with them?" Maddy asked. "Maybe they can help us."

I felt around inside myself: I was nervous about everything, anxious for home, loaded with responsibility for Maddy, and curious about the otter-people. They didn't seem particularly friendly, but they didn't seem scary either. "How does it feel to you?" I asked Maddy.

"Kind of weird, but safe."

"Then let's go," I said. If Maddy and I both felt okay about going with them, maybe it would be all right.

We followed the otter-people along the river until we reached a smaller river winding down a side valley.

Eneirda led us upstream, away from the highway in the human world. I kept checking behind me, worried about leaving the only place I recognized. But the walk was beautiful. Sunlight danced through the branches of the trees above us.

Maddy found muskberries near the path, and ate a few as we walked. When she spotted a big patch, she stopped to pick a handful.

"C'mon, Maddy," I called from the path. "They're almost out of sight."

"I'm coming," she said, as she picked a few more.

She poured half her berries into my hand. I popped some into my mouth; once again, energy flowed through my body. I felt like I was glowing, and suddenly, I could hear all the different sounds the water made as it tumbled over rocks and splashed into the air. I stopped for a moment, wondering what it would be like to paint when I felt like this.

Maddy and I had to run to catch up. We were panting when we reached the otter-people.

Eneirda turned, and with a look of horror, she hit my hand and sent the rest of my berries flying. She grabbed Maddy's hand, stained purple but empty, and looked at her mouth, purple-red at the corners. "*Ssst!* Muskberries not for humans!"

I gasped. "They're poisonous?"

"No, no," she said, as she saw our fear. "They are not poison." She sighed.

"Then why can't we eat them?" asked Maddy. "They're really good."

"Muskberries are for magic folk. *Sssst!* Only magic folk. Never for humans!" The way she said "humans" made it sound like a swear word.

She marched on ahead of us, faster than before, shoulders tense. Maddy and I followed, confused. Why couldn't we eat muskberries?

After walking a few more minutes, Eneirda and Arnica stopped on a gravel bar at the edge of the river and looked across to a clearing. Small otter-people wrestled and slid down a muddy slope, splashing into the water. When they saw us, warning cries and growls echoed, and they all dove out of sight.

Eneirda whistled three light calls, then a shrill squeal, and larger otter-people came out of caves along the far bank of the river. Slowly the small ones joined them on the shore. I counted eleven, in shades of brown and auburn, grey and gold. They watched us in stillness for a long time. Then the largest swam across the river and joined us on the pebble beach.

It was a little taller than me, with rich brown fur turned to grey at its head and across its shoulders, and amber skin. It looked at us closely, then spoke in a deep, resonant voice. "Who are you?"

"I'm Josh, and this is my sister Maddy. We're trying to get home."

"I am Greyfur. Why are you here?"

"Eneirda brought us."

He turned to Eneirda.

"Avalanche trapped Godren. Humans helped." I heard disgust in her voice again, when she said "humans." But then her eyes moved to Godren, and she smiled a little.

"*Tss*. How can you be in our world?" Greyfur asked.

"It's a long story," I started to say, just as Eneirda said, "They ate muskberries. *Sssst!*" That disgusted sound was back in her voice.

I didn't understand why she was making such a big deal about this. "Aleena said they were okay."

They drew back from us, hissing.

"What?" I asked. "What's wrong with eating muskberries?"

Greyfur sighed. "Muskberries help us connect to our magic."

"Why don't you want us to connect to your magic?" I asked.

"*Sssst!* Humans harm magic! But you saved Godren. You are welcome here. Sit. We will bring food."

We sat by the river. I rolled up my pants, and washed my leg. My calf was covered in dried blood, and a long gash was still oozing.

Greyfur drew Eneirda and Arnica away from us, and they chattered and whistled to one another. Finally, Arnica lifted Godren out of my hoodie, and she and Eneirda swam with him across the river. I tugged my hoodie over my head. It was still warm from Godren's body.

We watched Arnica carry Godren into one of the caves, followed by two otter-people. The rest gathered around Eneirda, and she spoke to them briefly. Then the otter-people scattered into caves and the forest. Soon they were back, swimming across the river with food balanced on large leaves. They spread a feast before us: small blue berries, icy water from the creek in a bark cup, mushrooms. Raw fish. Bugs laid out on leaves. A dead frog.

Eneirda squatted near us and gestured for us to eat. Our hands hovered over the food, trying not to offend, but not sure what to eat. I thought the berries would be safe. They were tasteless and filled with gritty seeds. We had a handful each, then drank water to wash them down. The cold water hurt my teeth.

Greyfur watched us. "*Tss*. You do not like our food?"

Maddy struggled to be polite. "It's very nice of you, but we don't eat bugs, or raw fish, or…or frogs."

Greyfur nodded. "We forget. Humans cook food," he told the others. "Light fire to cook. *Chrrr*." His purr was deeper than Eneirda's, a lower rumble.

Soon we were gulping down grilled meat. I was careful not to ask what it was. After more berries for dessert, we were full.

That's when Greyfur squatted in front of us, ready to talk. "Eneirda told of ring. What ring?"

"She was mistaken," I said. "There is no ring."

Greyfur gazed at me with large, dark eyes. It felt like standing in front of Mom, denying I'd done something wrong. I could never do it. I sighed. "Maddy, show him the ring."

She looked at me, puzzled. I nodded. Maddy slipped her hand into her pocket, then stretched it out to Greyfur, the ring on her finger. The otter-people peered at it, then drew back, hissing.

Greyfur spoke sternly. "*Sssst!* How do you have this? It is nexus ring."

"It's a long story," I said. "We found it."

Maddy poured out the story. "It was the troll's, then Aleena found it. She left it out to trap him, and I picked it up, and now she wants it back. The troll wants it too. But he's frozen into stone near the Spiral Tunnels, and Aleena is trapped with him."

The otter-people hummed and chattered, then turned back to us.

"Nexus ring harms our magic. *Sssst!*" Greyfur said. "You must leave now."

"Eneirda brought us here. We just want to get home!" I said.

"What of ring?"

"What about it? Do *you* want it, too?"

"We do not want it. *Sssst!* You must not keep it."

"What should we do with it?" I asked.

"Ring must go to giant at Castle Mountain," Eneirda said. "*Chrrr.* Only giant can keep it safe."

"Could you help us get home, then take the ring to the giant?" asked Maddy. She slid the ring off her finger and held it out.

Eneirda leapt back as if it would burn her, and the others hissed. "*Sssst!* I will not touch it. You must take it. You must set this right."

"Us?" we both squeaked. "To a giant?"

CHAPTER EIGHT

BOAT FITS STREAM

"**A** GIANT?" I SAID AGAIN, TRYING TO KEEP my voice steady. "We can't go to a giant. Giants are violent…mean…dangerous!"

Greyfur shook his head. "Is not violent. *Chrrrr.* You must take ring. Guarded ring must be."

"Aleena didn't say anything about the ring needing guarding," said Maddy.

"Aleena! *Sssst!*" Greyfur hissed. "Veil of magic separates our world from human world. Ring crossing between worlds tears veil. Troll and Aleena tear holes in veil. Now you, too! *Sssst!* Must stop. Ring must go to giant."

"We damaged the veil?" I asked. "When we crossed with Aleena?"

"Ring tears veil every crossing. Aleena told you not?"

"No," I said, then sighed. I suspected there were a lot of things Aleena hadn't told us.

"We only have…" I glanced at my watch, remembered it was useless here, and screwed up my eyes to think, "…maybe ten hours before the troll and Aleena could be after us again. We have to get home before then."

"Hurry, then, *tss*. Our world must not be harmed."

"But what about getting home?"

"Giant will help. First to giant, then home." He looked deep into my eyes, and nodded reassurance. "There is time. *Chrrr*. Go now."

What should we do? If we had damaged the veil, maybe we needed to make up for it. I shuddered, then said to Maddy, "I think we need to take the ring to the giant."

"Are you sure?" Maddy's voice quivered.

"No, I'm not sure. But if we give the ring to the giant, the troll and Aleena won't be interested in us any more. Then the giant can help us get home." I felt queasy saying that. I did *not* want to ask a giant for help!

But Greyfur looked at me with surprised approval. I felt like I do when Dad praises me, like I'd done something to be proud of.

"How do we get there?" I asked.

"I will paddle," said Eneirda.

Everyone turned to her. Greyfur held up his hand. "It will be difficult, *tss*, to take two over beginning of waters."

"It is necessary," she answered.

Somehow that was enough for the otter-people. One swam across the river and returned in an oval boat made of speckled grey bark stretched over a ring of branches. He handed Eneirda a little pouch of woven grasses on a knotted strap. Eneirda slipped it over her head. Then each otter-person stepped forward and touched her, forehead to forehead. It was eerie and solemn, and I wondered how difficult this was going to be.

Eneirda stepped into the boat, then held out a hand for Maddy. Once Maddy had settled beside her, I couldn't see how I could fit in with them. The boat was just too small. But Eneirda gestured to me. "*Chrrr*. Boat will be as big as we need."

That made no sense at all, but with all the otter-people watching, I stepped in and somehow, there was room for me to squeeze in beside Maddy. Eneirda knelt in front, pushed off, and began paddling upstream.

Water rushed past, leaping over rocks. Eneirda paddled softly, just enough to steer downstream on a quiet river. And yet we were travelling upstream on a mountain torrent. How was she doing it?

And how were we going to cross from the west side of the Rocky Mountains to the east side? Rivers don't cross the Continental Divide. Whatever stream we followed would get smaller and smaller until we reached its headwaters at the glaciers along the peaks of the Rocky Mountains.

"How are we going to get to Castle Mountain?" I asked. "If we follow the river, it will become too small for the boat. Then what?"

"Boat will be size we need, *tss*."

"Huh?" asked Maddy.

"For me, is small," she explained patiently. "For three, is bigger. For small water, is smaller. *Chrrr*. Just like paddle. Where we need go, paddle takes us. Upstream, downstream, no difference." She settled back to paddling as if that made everything clear.

It wasn't at all clear to me. "But what about where the river ends? I mean begins? Where water is melting off the glaciers?"

"Will paddle up glacier melts."

"But they're too small!"

"*Chrrr*. Boat will be size we need."

I tried to picture the three of us perched on a tiny boat.

Eneirda laughed and said, "We will fit. Safely we will cross:

Boat fit stream,
people fit boat,
paddle fit current."

I still didn't understand.

I dangled a hand in the river, then yanked it out. The water was as cold as ice. And the colour was changing. The river looked green on one side, and milky white on the other. I kept watching, and the colours separated further. "Maddy, look at the water. It's striped." Then I asked Eneirda, "What's going on?"

"Two rivers join. *Chrrr*. One white with glacier dust, one clear green."

"Which way do we go?" Maddy asked.

Eneirda lifted her paddle and pointed. "Ahead is meeting of waters, *tss*. We take clear river."

I could see two rivers joining. On the left was a milky white river, broad and slow. To the right, clear green water tumbled down a waterfall, wild and narrow. She wanted us to go up that? My heart leapt up my throat. "How can we go up a waterfall? Surely the other way will be easier."

"If take easy way, will reach falling water. In human world, Takakkaw Falls. So steep, water falls as mist, *tss*. Even this boat cannot rise straight up. Even this paddle cannot pull through mist."

I stared at the churning water ahead of us. "But how can we survive that?" Maddy was staring too, and I felt her small fingers lock around mine.

Eneirda stopped in the pool below the waterfall, using her paddle to hold us steady. "Boat and paddle are magic. *Chrrr*. It is necessary. Ring is only safe with giant."

"But why?" asked Maddy.

"Giant at Castle Mountain has one desire, *tss*, to protect magic world. He protects best by guarding nexus ring. If giant keeps ring, it cannot tear veil, and magic cannot leak into human world. *Chrrr.*"

"Magic leaking into our world?" I said. "That would be fantastic!"

"*Sssst!* Humans destroy magic. We would have less and less, and become like you."

I thought about how beautiful this world was, and compared it to our world. Maybe they did need to protect their magic from us.

Eneirda positioned the boat in the green stripe of water, paused a moment, then headed straight up the waterfall. Maddy fell back and screamed as the boat tilted upwards. I grabbed her, and we clung to the sides of the boat. Eneirda, perched in front, reached up into the waterfall to paddle. I tried not to look down at the water smashing at the base of the falls. Up and up we went, gasping in fear, icy water splashing us, numbing our hands. And then with a thud the boat leveled out, and we were above the waterfall.

As Maddy and I settled back, shaking and queasy, Eneirda kept paddling. We dashed between rocks and twisting roots, and ducked under fallen trees. The air grew colder and sharper, and gradually the trees thinned and became gnarled. I knew stunted trees grew in alpine areas, twisted by wind and snow, but they're usually small, and these were huge. And then I realized the stream was a tiny creek now, winding through rocky slopes, surrounded by small, stunted trees. And we had shrunk. The boat fit the stream, and we fit the boat, just like in Eneirda's poem.

I showed Maddy, and after a shocked look around, she snuggled close against my shoulder. Together we watched the stunted trees pass by. For a long time I thought about how to recreate this in a series of paintings. Then I noticed Maddy trembling.

"What are you thinking about?"

She whispered, face white, "Fee, Fie, Foh, Fum! I smell the blood of an Englishman."

I shuddered. "Don't say that. Don't even think it." But now that she had said it, all I could think about was Jack and the Beanstalk, and the giant who wanted to eat him. I looked around to try to take my mind off crunching bones.

We were crossing a high mountain meadow spotted with bright flowers. Beyond it, I could see mountain range after mountain range, snow patches catching the evening sun. The creek became smaller, the air thinner, and still Eneirda paddled. Soon snowbanks surrounded us and then, around a twist in the creek, we faced a wall of ice.

"Beginning of waters," Eneirda said. "River begins with glacier melting. Glaciers grow in winter, shrink in summer. Now shrink more than grow. *Ssst!* Down this valley glacier once reached."

Looking at the meadow below us I could imagine a spur of ice stretching down.

"Why is it melting?" Maddy asked.

Eneirda scowled. "*Sssst!* Humans light many fires. Even warms our world. Now glaciers melt."

I turned away from her scornful eyes.

We headed up the face of the glacier. I helped Eneirda navigate smaller and smaller trickles of water. Finally, she grounded the boat.

I stepped out first, and as soon as my weight was off the boat, I started to grow. I felt like an elastic as my arms and legs stretched. Soon I was normal size, looking down at doll-like Maddy and Eneirda in a toy boat. I held it steady while they climbed out, and soon they were normal size too.

"We walk now," Eneirda said. "We walk to water flow on other side."

I had hoped I could carry the boat in my pocket, but it grew as soon as I took it out of the water. I lifted it onto my shoulders as Maddy and Eneirda started up the ice.

Walking on the glacier was slippery, like crossing a skating rink tilted uphill, but it sounded like crunching across hard snow. There were deep cracks in the ice, big enough for a person to fall into. As soon as I started walking, I realized how high we were. I was warmer, moving, but short of breath and lightheaded.

I hurried to catch up with Eneirda, tipping the boat to one side so I wouldn't hit her. "Will we be okay at this altitude?"

She just looked at me, puzzled.

"We're really, really high," I said. "The air is thinner. Will we be okay here?"

Eneirda nodded. "Forget. High altitude bothers humans. *Tss*, where do you live? Near ocean? Or in high place?"

"Well, Calgary's pretty high. Not like this, but way higher than sea level."

"Fine, then."

But it didn't feel fine. This was the hardest I'd ever worked.

As I struggled up the ice, I looked around. Mountain peaks surrounded us, lit by golden sunlight. A constant wind whistled in my ears and chilled the sweat on my skin.

Eneirda spoke softly. "Many dangers here. *Tss*, be quiet inside. Magic will guide us."

The low sun cast shadows in the deep cracks waiting to swallow us. I peered into a crevasse and gulped. If we fell into that, we'd never get out. I was scared, but fascinated too. The ice inside the crevasse was a deep blue; I gazed down, wondering how I could capture that translucent blue on paper.

As we climbed I could feel sweat dripping down my back, then freezing in the cold wind. Maddy looked blue, from cold or maybe lack of oxygen. I finally noticed how quiet she'd been, ever since I'd decided we would go to the giant. But it wasn't the giant that was scaring me right now. A chant kept echoing in my head: *Troll in the morning, troll in the morning.*

And then I slipped stepping over a crevasse. As I slid, fear blazed through my body and somehow propelled my legs in a great leap to safety. Then I stood, clinging to the boat, panting and waiting for my heartbeat to slow.

Eneirda's lips tightened as she glanced at me with a look that reminded me of how she said "humans." I looked away.

She touched my arm. "Quiet your mind must be, *tss*. Human minds always busy. You must stop. Maddy is quiet."

Sure, because she's terrified, I thought. And then I slipped again.

"*Sssst!* You must listen! Let muskberries help. Look from inside."

"I don't see with my insides. I see with my eyes, and my hands."

"How see with your hands?"

"Well, I sort of feel what I'm drawing."

"*Chrrr.* Then see with hands. Be still inside. Let fingers guide you."

I groaned. She was as crazy as Mom. But then my feet slid out from under me and I collapsed as my legs dropped into a crevasse. Maddy and Eneirda leapt forward and pulled me out, then Maddy hung on to the boat to stop it from sliding away.

Once I was standing again, Eneirda stood in front of me, arms folded. "*Ssst!* If cannot, will be dead."

Dead? Oh, come on! But the look on her face was deadly serious. I gulped. She meant it! Maddy was frowning at me too. I made a face back, then remembered her dragging me out of the path of the avalanche. She saved my life then, and I promised to get her home.

Okay, I thought, *I can be quiet*. I took a deep breath, then another. Then I concentrated on my fingers. I imagined drawing the glacier, the crevasses, the deep blue shadows, sun gleaming off the ice. I felt a surge of energy, like when I ate muskberries. And suddenly I knew where to step, as if I was connected to the glacier somehow.

Eneirda looked pleased for just a moment, then she turned and walked on. I kept breathing and drawing in my head, and we kept climbing up the glacier. Then we reached the top, and I thought, *Hey, I did it! I haven't been falling!*

And then my feet slid out from under me and I crashed down, dropping the boat. It slid away from me, and I scrambled to grab it before it slipped down a crevasse. I tried to settle myself again. As long as I focused on my fingers, and not on the troll or the giant or my pride, my feet seemed to know where to go.

The setting sun lit the sky in peach and orange and pink. Even the blue shadows were warmed by it. The sun sets around 9:30 in late July in this part of the human world; I wondered if it was the same here.

As we climbed down the east side of the glacier, we could hear a trickle of water. Eneirda started searching for a stream. Past the edge of the glacier, I could see ground-up rock everywhere, as if someone had dumped thousands of truckloads of fine-ground gravel, fist-size rocks, and large boulders. They were in all colours – lots of greys, but browns and oranges too, greens and blue-greys. I could see the same colours in the rocks in the surrounding mountains. Blue-grey on one mountain, rusty orange on another, greys and tans. I took another mental snapshot, determined to paint this.

Eneirda spotted a trickle of water cutting through the ice, winding its way down the mountainside. When I set the boat in the water, it shrank to fit the tiny stream, then each of us shrank as we stepped into the boat. I was the last in and I worried I'd sink the boat. But as I shifted my weight, I began to shrink. My skin tightened and squeezed, and everything around me grew as I settled into the boat.

Breathing was easier once we were smaller. We cheered as we slid off the edge of the ice into a creek. The creek was small but wild, crashing over rapids, flinging us with it. But somehow Eneirda slowed us with her paddle, and as we flew down the side of the mountain, the creek became wider and calmer. It must have been a hot day; the air was warm and the sky clear as the sun set. But the setting sun didn't reach down the east-facing slope, and soon we were travelling in the shadow of the mountain.

"How long can we keep going?" I asked. "Can you see in the dark?"

Eneirda kept paddling. "*Chrrr.* River will guide us."

Trees closed in above us, and we travelled through gloom and then total darkness. The stream grew larger, and as it grew, the boat grew. I could feel my arms and legs stretching, but no matter how hard I stared, I couldn't see them change.

Eneirda said she would drop us off at the base of Castle Mountain, but how were we to climb it in the dark, before the troll and Aleena came after us? This was our second night away from Mom and Dad; they'd be frantic. I couldn't believe that the Shadows would fool them for long.

Maddy and I sat silently, listening to the sounds of the forest and watching the water. We could hear paddle splashes and Eneirda's breathing, an owl call startling us out of the silence. I blinked as my eyelids drooped and grew scratchy.

Then I spotted a shadow. "Look out!"

The boat slammed to a stop, filled with icy water and tipped. I was flung into the river. Water filled my nose and my lungs were bursting. I struggled to the surface, coughing and numb.

I looked frantically for Maddy. I couldn't see anything in the dark. "Maddy?" I yelled. "Maddy?"

I heard choking, and flailed around. Something soft brushed my hand. A pigtail. I grabbed it and pulled Maddy close, then swam sideways to the current. We swept up against a tree trunk fallen over the water.

I pushed Maddy ahead of me, then climbed out of the water and collapsed on a pebbly shore. We huddled together, shivering, as we peered into the darkness, looking for Eneirda, the boat, the paddle.

CHAPTER NINE

BEFORE DAWN

MADDY AND I STAGGERED OUT OF THE river, gasping and numb, but soon I could feel the warmth of the magic world wrapping itself around me. We were still shivering in wet clothes, but at least we weren't in danger of hypothermia.

"Eneirda, Eneirda," Maddy and I shouted. "We're over here."

I could only hear water rushing. What if Eneirda was drowning? Should I go back in? I knew I couldn't, not in the dark, not back into that icy water, with Maddy here, depending on me.

I couldn't see a thing. The sky was a deep teal blue, speckled with stars, but there was no moon. Even in this magic world, I couldn't see by starlight alone.

We kept calling and finally, we heard a faint call back. "Eneirda?"

"Here," she answered.

I listened carefully to the direction of her voice. "I think she's across the river." I shouted, "We're over here. Do you have the boat?"

"No boat," she called back. "Ankle hurt. Cannot swim."

Eneirda hurt? No boat? I leapt up, arms waving around me. "The troll will be coming for us by dawn. And when he's free, Aleena will be too. What are we going to do?"

"F-f-first, we n-need to get d-dry," Maddy said, teeth chattering.

"And how are we going to do that? Do you have any matches?"

"Humans," I heard Eneirda grumbling. "Fur easier than clothing. I have firestone," she called.

"We can't come across to you, and you're too hurt to swim to us," I said.

"I can throw. Can you catch?"

"But firestone is magic. I can't do magic."

"You ate muskberries?"

"Yes," I said.

"You crossed glacier, saw with fingers?"

"Yes," I said, puzzled.

"Then can use firestone. I will throw it."

My heart skipped a beat. Me? Do magic? "How will I see it?"

"Be quiet inside. Firestone gleams. Feel for it with fingers."

Oh no, not that again. I took a deep breath, then tried to feel catching the firestone. When I could imagine its cool softness in my palm, I decided I was as ready as I was going to be. I called out, "Okay, can you tell where I am from my voice?"

"Yes. Catch now."

I could almost see it glinting over the river. I reached up and felt it graze my hand, but I missed. I heard a splash. Maddy plunged a hand into the water and came up with a fistful of rocks. One of them shone at me in the moonlight. "I have it," I called back. "Now what?"

"Collect dry wood. Find safe place."

Shivering, Maddy and I groped for dry branches. I found a gazillion needles, most of them poking into my knees, but I found dry wood too. We cleared a spot near the river, laid a base of dry moss, and set small twigs nearby.

"We're ready," I called out.

"Josh make fire," Eneirda called back.

Oh sure, I thought. How was I supposed to do that? I held the firestone in my icy hand, a round blackness with threads of gleaming gold.

"Let mind be quiet. Let fingers feel magic. Find thread to pull."

Was she kidding? Do magic, with hands trembling so badly I couldn't hold the firestone still? But

I could try. I took a couple of deep breaths, trying to settle inside. Except I kept worrying about the troll, Aleena, the giant, the boat, Maddy, Eneirda, Mom and Dad.

I took another breath, and energy pulsed through my body, steadying my hands. I focused on the fire-stone. My eyes must have adjusted to the darkness, because I could see the stone more clearly. I reached out to touch it and could feel a thread. It was hot, but it didn't burn me.

I gently grabbed the tip of the thread and tugged it out of the stone. It was like pulling a loose thread from a button. I dangled it from my fingers over the dried moss, and when it touched, fire flared up the thread. I dropped it, and the moss began to smoulder. I carefully added twigs, then, as the fire grew, small branches. Maddy and I wiggled out of our wet jeans and runners, hoodie and fleece, then huddled close to the fire.

"Good work," Eneirda called. "Better now?"

"Much b-better," Maddy answered. "Are you okay?"

"Ankle is hurt. Will heal. Boat is smashed. Lost."

"Oh no!" Maddy cried out.

"How far are we from Castle Mountain?" I asked.

"Hours by boat. Without, too far for small humans."

"How close are we to people?"

"For human help must cross to human world. Would humans take you to Castle Mountain?"

I shook my head. "No way. They'd take us to the police, who would call our parents. We'd never get to Castle Mountain."

"Then I will not help you to human world. You must take ring to giant."

"But how? How do we get there?" Frustration made my body tight.

"Find boat. Fix it. Maybe. In morning we will know."

"But the troll could be looking for us by dawn!" I could hear the fear in my voice. "And you're hurt."

"Only ankle hurt. Can paddle. Still need boat. Morning is time to know. Need light to see."

When our clothes were dry, and Maddy and I were well roasted by the fire, we curled up and tried to sleep. My body was exhausted, but my mind kept racing. I didn't feel any of Eneirda's sureness or patience. Finally I dozed, stirring at every owl hoot and twig crack.

I WOKE AT DAWN. A quarter moon was rising in a clear sky. I peered around, wondering if the troll was nearby. He could be anywhere now, except in sunlight. Maddy was curled up against me, small and soft. I built up the fire. We jumped around to get warm, then pulled on our damp runners.

Eneirda was sitting on the far bank of the river, with one foot in the water. She called to me, "Humans sleep late. Is time to look for boat." I could hear her words, but no whistles or purring over the sound of the river.

I spotted the place we crashed. We'd hit a rock sticking out of the water, just in front of a fallen tree stretching out over the river. If we'd hit the tree, it would have been our heads that smashed. I felt sick imagining what might have happened.

I climbed all around the tree, then began searching downstream. No boat. Maddy scrambled under the tree, and didn't come out.

"Maddy," I called.

I heard a muffled, "Under here."

Maddy's hand waved from below the trunk. I lay down to peer under. She was wiggling through branches, trying to see into the water.

"What are you doing?"

"I wondered if the boat could be caught under here."

I tugged off my clothes, then slipped into the water and stood gasping at the cold. I knew it wasn't as numbingly cold as it would be in the human world, but it was still painful. I pulled myself along the tree, then ducked underneath. I groped around, pushing my way past a tangle of branches, and then I saw it. "It's here, Maddy! Climb out on the tree and help me."

She wiggled along the trunk above me, then helped me pull the boat out of the branches. I tugged it to shore, then struggled up the bank, stiff from the cold. Maddy inspected the boat while I dripped and shivered and huddled by the fire.

"Josh, one of the branches is smashed. They're tied together in a circle, and bark is lashed to the branches. I don't think it will float."

"Water noisy. Speak louder," Eneirda called from across the river.

Maddy repeated what she'd told me.

"Can be fixed. Need willow. Grows near water. Long, narrow leaves, thin branches. Cut three."

Maddy picked loose the lashings along the broken branch while I dressed, then searched the riverbank for willow. I couldn't see anything that looked right. I kept walking and worrying about the troll and what we'd do if we couldn't fix the boat. A branch slapped against my face. I looked at it and started to laugh. Long narrow leaves, growing near water – it must be willow. I tore off three long shoots, then ran back to Maddy.

Eneirda talked us through setting the branches around the rim and lashing them into place. The repair was sloppy and weaker than the rest of the branches, but good enough. Fast was more important than pretty, right now.

"Okay, what next?" I called across to Eneirda.

"Josh paddle here."

"You want me to paddle? I've paddled a canoe a few times, but not in a mountain river, without a life jacket or a parent."

"Or a paddle," said Maddy.

"What?"

"Where's the paddle? We didn't find it with the boat."

"Eneirda, do you have the paddle?"

"Paddle here. Find another."

"We're not going to just find a paddle!"

"Look around. See what land offers."

I glanced around. Trees. Bushes. Rocks. Maddy and I walked along the river's edge.

"Would this work?" Maddy held up an old log, with a deep split down the length of it. I tried to pull the two pieces apart, but they wouldn't budge. I grabbed a branch, and wedged it into the crack. Maddy leaned on the branch with me, and together we opened the split in the log. With a great CRACK, it broke, and we tumbled backwards.

I picked up the smaller of the two pieces, and walked back to the boat. "Will this do?" I asked Eneirda, waving it in the air.

"Will work. No magic in that paddle. Walk upstream. Current fast. Paddle hard, straight across."

We hauled the boat upstream until we reached a waterfall. I set the boat in a pool below the falls, and held it while Maddy climbed in. I steadied myself with the paddle across the sides of the boat while I sat, then pushed off into the current.

It grabbed the boat and swept us downstream before

I could get the paddle into the water. The round boat spun as I struggled, splashing water over both of us. I paddled furiously towards the far shore, but it seemed hopeless as the current carried us away. By the time I had a paddling rhythm, we could see Eneirda. We'd surged past her before we got near her shore.

"Look out!" Maddy yelled.

We were heading straight for a huge rock. The current swept past it in a rush. I flung my weight into the paddle and spun us out of the current into a backwater on the far side of the rock. From there, I paddled to shore. Then I carried the boat back to Eneirda. We had to struggle through the trees along the shore of the river, but walking was much better than paddling.

Eneirda smiled when she saw us. "Brave work. *Chrrr.* I paddle now."

I handed Eneirda her firestone, and she slipped it into the pouch hanging around her neck. Maddy grabbed the magic paddle, then held the boat steady while I helped Eneirda into it. Soon we were floating again. I could feel the tension in Eneirda's body as she paddled, faster than yesterday.

I reached up and touched the soft fur on her shoulder. "We've faced the troll before. We'll be okay."

She shivered. "Hate him. *Sssst!*" Never want to see him." She paddled on.

"Do you think the troll and Aleena are free yet?" asked Maddy.

I glanced at her. She looked pale. "Probably," I said. "But he can't follow us on the water."

"Aleena can," Maddy said softly.

I nodded and swallowed.

With morning light we could see more clearly. The river was widening, milky green from glacial runoff. We watched sunshine touch the mountain peaks to the west, then creep down the mountainsides until it lit the river in blinding light. Eneirda paddled faster.

Finally I spotted Castle Mountain. Wolf willow grew along low grassy banks. Trees were more scattered as we moved into the wide meadows of the Bow Valley.

"How will you get home after you drop us off?" I asked.

"*Chrrr*. Getting far from troll will make it easy."

"Will the boat hold together?" Maddy asked. "Won't you be tired?"

"Will reach home. No hurry, *tss*. *You* must hurry. Follow animal trail straight to mountain. You must find giant."

Eneirda paddled the boat to shore, stopping beside a fallen log. I could see Maddy didn't want to say goodbye, torn between worry for Eneirda and fear of what lay ahead. Finally, she touched fingers with Eneirda and turned away, brushing a hand across her cheek. I didn't know what to say either. Eneirda reached out and we touched fingers.

"Thank you," I whispered. "Thank you, and be careful."

"You must give ring to giant, *tss*. That is thanks I need." And she was gone, paddling upriver, heading back to the glaciers.

CHAPTER TEN

CASTLE MOUNTAIN

MADDY AND I STOOD ON THE BANK OF the Bow River, looking up at the sheer cliffs of Castle Mountain. Dark storm clouds were building across the valley. Why couldn't it stay sunny? The troll and Aleena could be here any moment. Maybe they were here already! I spun around, watching for movement. I didn't know which was worse – meeting the troll and Aleena, or finding a giant.

Maddy spotted a faint trail winding across a meadow. It led us into a matchstick forest of tall evergreen trees with bare trunks and low ground cover. We hiked through the morning coolness, stomachs grumbling. But even if we'd had food, I was too anxious to choke down a single bite.

We followed the trail up the forested base of Castle Mountain. It towered over us, striped in horizontal layers and vertical crevices. The path led us higher, up the flank of the mountain. We walked slowly, while I watched and listened.

I heard a rumbling, then another, and another, regularly spaced. Maddy reached for my hand and we stood on the path listening.

"Maybe it's the giant," Maddy whispered.

I didn't know if I wanted her to be right or not. I had a really bad feeling about this. We stepped around a curve in the path and there was the troll, standing with his feet planted wide, his arms crossed, fuming.

Maddy and I froze. We stood staring up the path, the troll glowering down at us. His gaze shifted behind us, and his lips curled in a nasty smile. I glanced back; there was Aleena, cloak swirling. They each took a step closer to us, Aleena from below, the troll from above. Maddy shivered and moved closer to me. It was like they had agreed to work together, to stop us from taking the ring to the giant. Afterward, I guessed their fight would go on. My stomach churned.

Another step from above and below narrowed the trap. I thought frantically, trying to find a way out. Maybe we could run, but could Maddy run fast enough? Could I? I felt panic rising up my throat as I heard Aleena and the troll each take another step.

I grabbed Maddy's hand and pulled her off the path, into the forest. We dashed through the trees. I could hear the troll crashing through the brush behind us. I figured Aleena was moving silently, and probably faster. We raced to the left, then up the mountain, branches slashing our faces. Maddy stumbled; I caught her around the shoulders and together we ran on.

And then we were out of the trees, in a clearing high on the side of the mountain. That's when I realized the rumbling continued, regular, deep thuds. Soon I could feel it through the earth. They were footsteps. It had to be the giant!

The troll was panting up from below, Aleena closing in from the right. I didn't know what to do, just that I wanted to be somewhere, anywhere, else. I picked up a piece of wood, a heavy club.

"Give me the ring," I whispered to Maddy.

She slipped it off her finger and handed it to me. I closed my fist around the ring, squeezing tight. Then Maddy took the club from me, raised it above her shoulders like a baseball bat, and said, "I'll protect you from behind."

I stared at her, all four feet and forty-four pounds of her. *Yeah, right*, I thought. And then I looked in her eyes. She had this look I'd never seen before, of such determination. "Smack the first one that comes near us," I said.

She nodded, and we stood back to back, waiting and listening.

I could hear them both, Aleena panting lightly, the troll breathing in raspy gasps. They stepped closer to us, one from below, one from the side. Then another step. Maddy tightened her grip on the club.

The troll roared and charged at us. Maddy swung the club and he ducked. Aleena moved in from the side, and Maddy turned back and forth, swinging the club at both of them.

The rumblings deepened into solid thuds I could feel in my feet and up my legs. I could smell rock dust as the pounding moved around the face of the mountain. And there was the giant, looming over us. He must have been twice as tall as my dad, solid as a column of stone. His skin was grey and creased like the mountain, and his face was still as a rock, watching us.

When he saw the troll and Aleena, his face scrunched up like he was smelling something disgusting. He bellowed, in a voice that shook the mountain, "Who brings vermin to my castle?"

I stood frozen with fear, like a troll turned to stone. Maddy nudged me and I shook myself. I held out the ring in the palm of my hand. The giant's eyes widened when he recognized it.

The troll stepped closer, behind me, only held off by Maddy and her club. He spoke in a wheedling voice, "It's *my* ring. If you give it to me, I won't hurt you." He held out his hand, meaty and grasping. When I didn't react, he seemed to puff himself up to look larger and enormously threatening.

Then Aleena spoke, her voice soft and gentle. "Don't trust that evil troll. Give me the ring and I'll take you to your parents." She held out a delicate hand. "You can trust me," she said. But I knew I couldn't.

I turned to look up at the giant, expecting him to ask too. He just stood there, rock solid. "Why should I give you the ring?" I asked.

He stared down at me, a huge block. I shut my eyes so I didn't have to see him. Then I heard him speak, in a deep rumble. "I will keep it safe."

"That's it?" I asked, angry at being surrounded by three monsters. "'I will keep it safe'? No threats, no magic, no persuasions?"

"You must decide," he replied.

I turned to Maddy, guarding me with the club. "Maddy, what should I do?"

Before she could answer, the troll bellowed, "Not her! *You* must decide!" He raised his arms towards the mountainside and a huge rock floated down. It stopped, hovering, above Maddy's head. "If she speaks, I will drop the rock!"

The giant frowned and stepped forward, then stepped back again as the rock shifted above Maddy. She stood rigid, not even breathing, eyes staring up at the rock.

I could feel my whole body shaking. I felt sick, but I took a deep breath, trying to listen inside.

Then Aleena spoke. "Josh, give me –"

"Silence!" roared the giant.

The sound was so loud it hurt my ears. Everyone became silent and stared at the ring nestled in my hand. Even though the otter-people had told me to give the ring to the giant, it seemed impossible that I could trust this block of rock. But a sureness was growing deep inside of me.

I whipped my arm back, and threw the ring up to the giant.

The troll yelled, "NO!" and launched himself up the mountain, arms reaching to catch the ring as it fell. Maddy jumped to the side, away from the rock plummeting to the ground where she'd been standing. Aleena followed the troll, grabbing for the ring, the troll, anything. The ring spun high into the air, then curved down, too soon, down towards the troll's grasping fingers.

At the last moment the giant reached out and closed his great hand over it. The troll and Aleena both cried out, "No!"

The troll stood above us, looking from Maddy and me to the giant, his face dark red with anger. He opened his mouth to speak, but no sound came out. He raised his fist and bellowed as he launched himself at us.

The giant thudded down the mountainside and spoke, his voice like thunder. "Troll, be gone."

The troll slowed but kept coming. The giant reached out with his enormous arm and plucked the troll from the path. The giant held the troll up to his face and whispered a rumbling, "Be gone, troll, or I will hold you up until the clouds leave and the sun shines on you."

He dropped the wriggling troll below us, and Gronvald slunk into the woods, curses and threats drifting back to us. "I'll get it back. It's my ring. I'll teach you to mess with me."

Aleena stood gazing at us with a look of fury and loss all mixed together, then turned and glided down the mountain.

Now, it was just Maddy, the giant and me.

The giant was enormous. His face was craggy, with deep, shadowed furrows. His hair and eyes and clothes were as grey as Castle Mountain. His hands were huge, and looked like they'd been roughly chiseled from stone. And yet they were gentle hands. I studied him, and decided I'd draw him with a hard medium-grey pencil, sharpened so I could get all the angles, but in a softer colour than Aleena or the troll.

The giant peered at the ring. "Nexus ring," he said. "Yours?" and he looked at me. His voice was deep and rumbly, and he spoke slowly, as if he needed a long time to think before speaking.

Maddy cleared her throat. "It…it's mine. But I don't want it. I want you to keep it safe."

"I am Keeper. I will keep it safe," replied the giant.

"What's your name?" I asked.

"I am Keeper," he said, in his slow, deep voice.

"But what is your name?" I said. "What do people call you?"

"People call me 'Aaah! A giant!' Then they run away."

"Josh," Maddy interrupted.

"Just a minute, Maddy," I said.

"Maybe he doesn't have another name." She turned to the giant. "May we call you Keeper?"

"I would be honoured," he replied, bowing his head. Then he asked, "How did you get the ring?"

"It's a long story," I said.

I must have sounded tired, because Keeper answered, "Come to my castle, and tell me your story. I like stories."

His castle? No way. "Uh," I said, "we need to get home."

Keeper leaned down to me, trying to concentrate, I think, but it was unnerving having him so close. I swallowed. "The otter-p…" my voice cracked and I had to repeat myself. "The otter-people said you could help us get home. We don't know how to cross the veil back to our world."

The giant smiled. "You returned the nexus ring. I will help you. First we must go to my castle. So you will know the ring will be safe."

"Is it very far?" asked Maddy.

Keeper peered down at her and nodded. "You are tired. I will carry you."

He patted his shoulder, then leaned down near me. When I realized he wanted me to sit on his shoulder, my stomach slid into my feet. I stared up at Keeper, shocked. His face lit up in a huge rocky grin and he nodded. I gulped, then scrambled onto his right shoulder. Then he reached for Maddy.

"Are you sure?" she asked me, looking wary.

I did a quick sketch on my leg, of Maddy and the giant and me, and it was light and funny and safe. I nodded to Maddy. "Come on up." And then I didn't feel safe at all, as Keeper bent down to pick up Maddy. I grabbed his head to hang on to. He settled Maddy on his left shoulder, and started walking, his footsteps reverberating up the mountain.

It was like I'd imagine riding an elephant to be, high and swaying, and very scary. But soon I forgot how I was moving, as my eyes widened at all the things I'd never seen before: the forest from high in the trees, eye to eye with birds in their nests. When the trees opened up, I had an incredible view across the valley. Quietly I sketched across my pant leg.

Maddy swayed with Keeper's walk, one hand clasping his hand and the other in his hair to steady herself. She looked nervous, but excited too. We grinned at each other.

Keeper walked out of the trees at the base of a cliff. Castle Mountain rose straight above us. I almost fell off when Keeper swept his arm across the face of the mountain.

"My castle," he announced.

Maddy gaped. "How do you get into it?"

"Watch," he said, and a slow grin spread across his face. He climbed a series of rock steps, then followed a ledge along the face of the cliff. Lucky Maddy was against the cliff wall. I was on the outside edge. I hoped she didn't notice me clinging to Keeper's head. I couldn't look down.

With a jerk, Keeper stopped and bent over. I slid off his shoulder in a weak-kneed stagger. Maddy wobbled beside me. We were facing a deep crack in the mountain. "I can not carry you here. It is too narrow."

Inside the crack were rock steps so big no human would recognize them. We started climbing, Keeper boosting us up the steps we couldn't scramble over. Soon Maddy and I were sweaty and filthy. We kept climbing, struggling up the giant steps, trying to stay ahead of Keeper's enormous hands pushing us up.

And then we were through, behind the face of Castle Mountain.

CHAPTER ELEVEN

KEEPER

KEEPER SWUNG US BACK ONTO HIS shoulders and kept walking, on a path winding up to the peak of Castle Mountain. When we reached the top we sat together, perched on the crest of the mountain.

We could see forever, down to the Bow River winding through meadows and across to the mountains ringing the valley. Dark clouds gathered around Storm Mountain, and wind pulled at our hair. Above us, an eagle soared.

Keeper reached into one of his deep pockets. "Are you hungry?" he asked.

Yes! Even more than sketching, I wanted to eat!

He held out two buns. In our hands, they were as

big as loaves of bread. As we tore open the bread, he chuckled and the sound reverberated like an actor's voice on a stage. "I have more buns. Eat. Eat!"

After we'd each devoured a loaf, Keeper said, "Now, tell me how you have the ring."

And so we told him. He listened carefully. When we were done he sat back and sighed. "That is a good story. I will keep the ring safe." He looked at Maddy. "Maddy liked it?"

"I did," said Maddy, a little mournfully. "But not any more."

"I have rings. You may choose one. Does Josh want a ring too?"

I shook my head. "No, thanks. I don't need a ring. I just want to get home."

Keeper nodded. "Come. I will show you where I will keep the nexus ring, and Maddy can choose a new one."

We climbed down from the peak, along ledges and giant steps, into a cave. It was cool and dark and very deep. I couldn't see to the end of it, even with Keeper's torch.

Through the dimness, I could see shelves carved into the walls, a bed piled with blankets, a huge wooden table with chairs of various sizes, and a big stone fireplace. It was hard to see details in the dim light; I longed to stay and explore. But Keeper led us deep into the cave, where he set his shoulder against a slab of rock and began pushing. The rock screeched as it slid across the floor of the cave. Keeper reached into a hollow underneath, and pulled out a worn grey bundle.

"Come see rings, little Maddy." Keeper opened the ragged cloth across one huge hand, revealing a dozen rings. "What do you like?"

Maddy looked carefully at them all. She tried on rings sparkling with jewels, but finally chose a small silver band engraved with a pattern of interlocking lines. "I like this. Is it safe?"

"This is a safe ring for Maddy. Elves made it." He wrapped the cloth into a tight bundle and placed it back in the hollow. "After I take you home, I will put the nexus ring here." Then he set his shoulder to the slab again, and slowly pushed it back into place.

"Will the ring be safe?" I asked.

"I am Keeper. It will be safe. Trolls do not like me."

"They might trick you again," Maddy said.

"They will not trick me again. Now, is it time to go home?"

"Yes," said Maddy. "I want to go home."

We sat outside the cave, watching eagles float above the peaks. Below us, the mountain curved down in a huge bowl, cradling a lake. Bear cubs tumbled in a meadow. Storm clouds moved off to the south, and we basked in the sun and talked about getting home.

"I know where we are," I said. "If we can cross over to our side of the veil, and go to the highway and stop someone, they'll take us to the police. And the police will call our parents."

"You want the police?" asked Keeper slowly. "Why not your parents?"

"Well, sure," I said, "I'd like to go straight home, but we can't. We've been missing for days." The troll's Shadows couldn't be convincing at home, joking at dinner and doing homework. "Mom and Dad will have called the police already."

"No," said Keeper. He paused for a moment, then explained. "Time shifts crossing the veil. I can fix it. Where would you like to meet them?"

"Aleena said that too. I don't understand. Human time is logical."

Keeper answered firmly, "Sometimes there is no logic. Sometimes it just is. I can fix it. Where would you like to meet your parents?"

"Okay. How about back at the Giant Cedars Boardwalk? Where this all started?"

"You saw them drive away?" Keeper asked. When I nodded, he said, "I cannot take you back to before they left, because you would still be there. And it would take us a long time to walk. Choose someplace closer."

Maddy spoke up. "Josh, you know that roadside pull-off where we stop on the way home, where we can just see Banff? Could we meet them there?"

"But what if they don't stop? And what about those Shadows in the back seat? And that was two days ago!"

"The troll makes trouble magic," Keeper said. "I make fixing magic. When you come, the Shadows will go. What time?"

I gave up. "Okay." I thought about Dad's schedule, and Mom's magic places. "How about when our parents stop at the Bow Valley Viewpoint, last Wednesday. The last Wednesday in July," I said, looking at Keeper. When he nodded, I kept going. "Around 3:30. No, a little earlier. We should get there first."

"How will you get us there without being seen?" Maddy asked.

"We will not cross the veil until we are nearby. Humans will not see us."

He hoisted us onto his shoulders and we set off down the mountain. We swayed with him, ducking to avoid branches, listening to chipmunks scolding. We stopped for a drink when we came to a stream, then followed it downhill.

When we reached the Bow River, Keeper lowered us to the ground and waded into the water. When we didn't follow him, he turned and gestured. "Come. We need to go down the river."

"What?" Maddy and I both squeaked.

"It's too cold," I said, shocked.

Keeper smiled. "It is a lovely afternoon for a swim."

Maddy and I just shivered. "It's too cold for us," I insisted.

Keeper stepped back to shore and looked down at

us. "I will keep you warm." Then he leaned down and blew. His breath surrounded us like a feather-soft blanket. Instead of vanishing, the air settled around us in a cocoon of warmth.

Then Keeper took our hands and led us into the river. I could feel the water rushing by my legs, soaking my clothes, but the cold couldn't penetrate the barrier Keeper had wrapped around me.

As the water tried to sweep us away, Keeper grabbed us, lay down on the water, and pulled us onto his chest. And that's how we floated down the Bow River, draped across Keeper's chest, legs dangling behind as the current carried us downstream.

"Hey, Josh," said Maddy, giggling, "you said you wanted to go rafting this summer. Bet you didn't think it would be like this!"

I laughed, thinking of all the rafts we'd watched floating down the Bow River in Calgary.

After a while I could see Mount Rundle, a wedge of rock slicing into the sky. I knew Banff sat at the base of Rundle, and that we could see both from the Banff Viewpoint. But we weren't close enough yet.

"In the human world there are lakes here," said Keeper, lifting his head slightly to look at us. "In the magic world the river winds back and forth. We can float downstream to near the doorway."

When Mount Rundle was as tall as I remembered it from the Banff Viewpoint, Keeper swam us to shore.

We stepped out into a marsh, soft and muddy underfoot. We squished past cattails and reeds, birds flying up around us. The air was fresh and cold, with a sweet smell like crushed rosemary.

Walking ahead of me, Maddy suddenly stopped and turned with her face scrunched up. "Ewwww. What is that disgusting smell?"

I stepped closer and it hit me too. The fresh sweet air was suddenly filled with the stench of rotten eggs.

Keeper turned and smiled. "Here," he said, and he led us around an open patch of water. He pointed to the water nearest a hillside; the surface was covered in grey-and-white slime, with leaves floating on top.

"Oh, that's really gross," I said.

Keeper laughed. "Warm water comes from inside the earth."

Maddy and I bent down and touched the water.

"Hey, it really is warm," Maddy said. "But why?"

"It's a hot spring," I said, finally understanding. "Just like in Banff. Remember how much it stinks there?"

"But why is that stuff growing here?"

"This algae likes warm water and sulphur," said Keeper. "It is happy here."

Maddy and I made faces at each other, then walked on along the base of the hillside.

Even with Keeper's blanket of warmth, we were still wet, and soon the mountain wind set us shivering.

When Keeper noticed, he stood us side by side with our arms up. He took a deep breath, filling his lungs with air, then blew on us, but with more and hotter air than his lungs could possibly hold. It was like standing under the hair dryer at the swimming pool, only bigger.

He twirled a finger in a circle for us to turn so he could dry us all around, and I laughed at what a delicate movement it was in such a huge hand.

When we were dry and warm, Keeper said, "Some doorways have been lost through human changes. But there is one close to your meeting place. I will open the doorway with the ring, we will cross to your world, and I will return." He looked sad.

"What's wrong?" Maddy asked.

"The ring should not be used, but I do not have enough magic without it. We will tear the veil twice. But you must get back to your world, and you do not have your own magic."

"I have some magic," I said. "Well, sort of. I used firestone."

His eyes widened, and he leaned closer to me. "How could you?"

I tried to explain. "Aleena fed us muskberries, and Eneirda taught me how to use my fingers to feel magic. And, well, I just did it."

Keeper smiled. "Maybe together we can work the magic we need." He held out the ring, tiny in his rocky hand, and Maddy and I each touched a finger to it.

Keeper closed his eyes for a moment, thinking, then spoke in his slow, deep voice. "Imagine a doorway, here in front of us. Breathe in imagining, breathe out mist."

I shut my eyes and tried to focus, but I couldn't concentrate. I kept thinking of Mom and Dad, and remembering the rock hanging over Maddy's head, and the taste of muskberries. But I couldn't focus on imagining a doorway.

Why couldn't I do this? I could use the firestone. I remembered the first touch of the thread of fire, and realized I needed to use my fingers.

Instead of trying to imagine the doorway, I sketched it. With a finger scratching against my pant leg, I drew a doorway like the one we'd gone through with Aleena. As I drew, I could feel energy building, and I pulled it into my lungs as I inhaled. When I exhaled, mist blew from my mouth and thickened into a white fog. And slowly a doorway formed in the mist.

The crags of Keeper's face shifted into an enormous grin. "You opened the doorway! You can cross without me!"

"Will we still cause a tear?" asked Maddy.

"No. Because Josh has magic, you can cross without me, without the ring. It is only the ring crossing that tears the veil."

Keeper looked carefully at my face. "Are you tired?" he asked.

"No, I'm fine," I said. "Why?"

"Magic folk get very tired opening a doorway." He looked puzzled.

I shrugged. "Well, I feel okay."

Keeper nodded slowly, then he smiled as he looked down at us. "You must cross now. Follow the animal trail up the hillside. There is a fallen tree pointing the way. Follow the trail to the tunnel for animals to walk under the highway."

"I remember the tunnel," I said. "It was built so animals wouldn't get killed crossing the road."

Keeper nodded.

"Will we meet a bear?" asked Maddy, eyes huge again.

"No. Big animals do not like tunnels," Keeper said. "Before the tunnel, turn left, walk to the fence, climb it, then walk to the highway viewpoint."

Tree pointing, animal trail, uphill, left at tunnel, climb fence. I didn't feel at all confident we could find the viewpoint, but I figured that as long as I could see Mount Rundle, I could at least find the highway.

Maddy reached up to hug Keeper, and he swept her into his arms. She looked like a doll, with her legs dangling. He held her tight and whispered, "Little Maddy." He tapped the silver ring on her finger. "This ring will help you see magic."

I tried to shake hands, but he pulled me close. "Josh, never forget the magic in you."

"Goodbye. Thank you," we said as we turned towards the doorway.

"Children returned the nexus ring. Keeper will never forget."

Keeper stood near the doorway while Maddy and I held hands and stepped in. Immediately, we were surrounded by fog. We looked back and couldn't see a thing. I could only hear whirring. I checked my watch; the hands were spinning wildly.

Ahead of us another doorway appeared in the mist, and we stepped through onto thick, tall grass on the shore of a small lake. Behind us, I could see nothing but the doorway and fog.

The lakeshore was peaceful by human standards, with wind blowing through the grasses, birds calling across the water, and the fragrance of mint drifting up as we walked. But the colours seemed muted and the air stale after the vibrancy of the magic world. Across the lake, I could hear a train engine whining and a lower-pitched thrumming of wheels on tracks. The radiance of magic was gone and I was already missing it.

"There's the fallen tree," said Maddy, pointing away from the lake.

I sighed. "Okay, let's go."

We walked to the tree, then let it point our way up the hillside. We found a path through the trees almost right away. As we followed it uphill, the trees changed from dancing-leaved aspen to dark spruce.

Maddy carefully stepped around some round black poops on the trail. "We're definitely on an animal path," she said. "I just hope Keeper was right about bears not liking the tunnel."

We spotted the highway above us and soon we could see a boxy tunnel under the highway. "Turn left," I said. "Isn't that what Keeper said?"

"Um, I think so," said Maddy, but she didn't look sure.

Great. We turned left, and soon came to a fence made of wire mesh stretched across green wooden frames and posts. "I hope this is the right place," I muttered.

"It is, it is!" shouted Maddy. "Look!"

She pointed up through the trees towards the highway. I couldn't see anything until I stood right behind her and spotted the wooden signs pointing to the mountains surrounding the viewpoint.

"That's it!' I said.

I have no idea why, but part of the fence was angled at forty-five degrees, so I just walked up the wire mesh, then swung myself over the top edge of wood and climbed down the post. Then Maddy walked up the fence and I helped her down.

We found another path on the other side, a human trail marked by scraps of garbage. The trail led us straight to the viewpoint. We followed the path to the end of a low stone wall and stepped around it as if we'd just been out for a walk. Maddy followed me down the sidewalk beside the wall. A tour bus pulled into the parking lot and soon we were surrounded by picture-snapping tourists. They oohed and ahhed over the view of Mount Rundle and the glimpse of Banff. Families and cyclists joined them, but our parents weren't there.

We sat on the wall, waiting in the sun. I watched for the van, then looked at the people around us. They kept glancing at us, then looking away. In spite of our trip down the river, we were filthy. I had torn and bloody jeans, and Maddy and I both had mud-caked runners, tangled hair, and berry-stained shirts. Maybe it would be best not to talk to anyone.

"Is it the right day?" Maddy asked.

"I don't know," I said. I checked my watch: 3:27. That seemed vaguely right for the angle of the sun. But how could we ask? "If we just sit here," I murmured to Maddy, "they'll ignore us, but if we ask the time and date, they'll start asking about our parents."

Then I remembered what Keeper had said. "Never forget the magic in you." I sat quietly, and felt with my fingers. Softly, I began to sketch on my jeans – where were they?

I tried to relax and just sketch, without thinking. My dirty fingers kept drawing a circle with eight flat sides. I couldn't figure out what it was, until I tried to quiet myself again, and realized it was a stop sign. Then my fingers added a long pole, and a woman in a hard hat leaning against it. I started to laugh.

Maddy turned to me. "What's so funny?"

"Construction delay," I said. "They'll be here soon."

We sat leaning against each other, watching the tourists file back onto their bus. Slowly it backed up and drove away. And then Mom and Dad pulled up to the curb. Maddy and I ducked out of sight and scooted over to the van. Just as Keeper had promised, as we neared the van the Shadows vanished.

"Wow, did you guys ever get out fast! I thought you were asleep." Those were Dad's first words to his missing kids. "I wish you were always this quiet. We made great time, except for that delay for highway construction near Golden. Just a bit behind schedule."

Then Mom said, "You two are filthy! How did you get so dirty at the Boardwalk? Baths for both of you as soon as we get back." She shook her head at us. Then she said, "Now that you've woken up, why don't we look for some magic to get us through the final veil of mist?"

Maddy and I looked at each other and grinned.

"No," I said, "we've had enough magic for now."

As we headed back to the van Maddy asked me, quietly, "We'll be home soon, won't we?"

"Yes," I said, "we're almost home."

ACKNOWLEDGMENTS

MANY THANKS TO EVERYONE WHO helped me become a better writer, and this a better story, especially Mr. Gayle, Terry Gilbert, Eileen Coughlan, Valerie Compton, Maggie de Vries, Richard Scrimger and Cathy Beveridge; to all my friends and family who read the manuscript and encouraged me; to Brenda Rudd who said, "Of course you're creative," and started it all; and to Barbara Sapergia at Coteau Books who rescued my story from the slush pile.

And more thanks to Laura Peetoom, for her careful editing, always aware of what the story needed; and to everyone at Coteau Books, who are a joy to work with.

ABOUT THE AUTHOR

M AUREEN BUSH has a Post-graduate Certificate of Creative Writing from Humber College. She also obtained a Bachelor's degree in History and a Masters in Environmental Design (Environmental Science), both from the University of Calgary. She is a trained mediator and public involvement consultant, and has written and edited in this field.

Born in Edmonton, Maureen Bush now lives in Calgary with her husband and two daughters.